A House to Let

Collins, Dickens, Gaskell, and Procter

A House to Let

The present edition is a reproduction of previous publication of this classic work. Minor typographical errors may have been corrected without note, however, for an authentic reading experience the spelling, punctuation, and capitalization have been retained from the original text.

ISBN: 978-1-64799-143-2

Contents

OVER THE WAY

I had been living at Tunbridge Wells and nowhere else, going on for ten years, when my medical man—very clever in his profession, and the prettiest player I ever saw in my life of a hand at Long Whist, which was a noble and a princely game before Short was heard of—said to me, one day, as he sat feeling my pulse on the actual sofa which my poor dear sister Jane worked before her spine came on, and laid her on a board for fifteen months at a stretch—the most upright woman that ever lived—said to me, "What we want, ma'am, is a fillip."

"Good gracious, goodness gracious, Doctor Towers!" says I, quite startled at the man, for he was so christened himself: "don't talk as if you were alluding to people's names; but say what you mean."

"I mean, my dear ma'am, that we want a little change of air and scene."

"Bless the man!" said I; "does he mean we or me!"

"I mean you, ma'am."

"Then Lard forgive you, Doctor Towers," I said; "why don't you get into a habit of expressing yourself in a straightforward manner, like a loyal subject of our gracious Queen Victoria, and a member of the Church of England?"

Towers laughed, as he generally does when he has fidgetted me into any of my impatient ways—one of my states, as I call them—and then he began,—

"Tone, ma'am, Tone, is all you require!" He appealed to Trottle, who just then came in with the coal-scuttle, looking, in his nice black suit, like an amiable man putting on coals from motives of benevolence.

Trottle (whom I always call my right hand) has been in my service two-and-thirty years. He entered my service, far away from England. He is the best of creatures, and the most respectable of men; but, opinionated.

"What you want, ma'am," says Trottle, making up the fire in his quiet and skilful way, "is Tone."

"Lard forgive you both!" says I, bursting out a-laughing; "I see you are in a conspiracy against me, so I suppose you must do what you like with me, and take me to London for a change."

For some weeks Towers had hinted at London, and consequently I was prepared for him. When we had got to this point, we got on so expeditiously, that Trottle was packed off to London next day but one, to find some sort of place for me to lay my troublesome old head in.

Trottle came back to me at the Wells after two days' absence, with accounts of a charming place that could be taken for six months certain, with liberty to renew on the same terms for another six, and which really did afford every accommodation that I wanted.

"Could you really find no fault at all in the rooms, Trottle?" I asked him.

"Not a single one, ma'am. They are exactly suitable to you. There is not a fault in them. There is but one fault outside of them."

"And what's that?"

"They are opposite a House to Let."

"O!" I said, considering of it. "But is that such a very great objection?"

2

"I think it my duty to mention it, ma'am. It is a dull object to look at. Otherwise, I was so greatly pleased with the lodging that I should have closed with the terms at once, as I had your authority to do."

Trottle thinking so highly of the place, in my interest, I wished not to disappoint him. Consequently I said:

"The empty House may let, perhaps."

"O, dear no, ma'am," said Trottle, shaking his head with decision; "it won't let. It never does let, ma'am."

"Mercy me! Why not?"

"Nobody knows, ma'am. All I have to mention is, ma'am, that the House won't let!"

"How long has this unfortunate House been to let, in the name of Fortune?" said I.

"Ever so long," said Trottle. "Years."

"Is it in ruins?"

"It's a good deal out of repair, ma'am, but it's not in ruins."

The long and the short of this business was, that next day I had a pair of post-horses put to my chariot—for, I never travel by railway: not that I have anything to say against railways, except that they came in when I was too old to take to them; and that they made ducks and drakes of a few turnpike-bonds I had— and so I went up myself, with Trottle in the rumble, to look at the inside of this same lodging, and at the outside of this same House.

As I say, I went and saw for myself. The lodging was perfect. That, I was sure it would be; because Trottle is the best judge of comfort I know. The empty house was an eyesore; and

3

that I was sure it would be too, for the same reason. However, setting the one thing against the other, the good against the bad, the lodging very soon got the victory over the House. My lawyer, Mr. Squares, of Crown Office Row; Temple, drew up an agreement; which his young man jabbered over so dreadfully when he read it to me, that I didn't understand one word of it except my own name; and hardly that, and I signed it, and the other party signed it, and, in three weeks' time, I moved my old bones, bag and baggage, up to London.

For the first month or so, I arranged to leave Trottle at the Wells. I made this arrangement, not only because there was a good deal to take care of in the way of my school-children and pensioners, and also of a new stove in the hall to air the house in my absence, which appeared to me calculated to blow up and burst; but, likewise because I suspect Trottle (though the steadiest of men, and a widower between sixty and seventy) to be what I call rather a Philanderer. I mean, that when any friend comes down to see me and brings a maid, Trottle is always remarkably ready to show that maid the Wells of an evening; and that I have more than once noticed the shadow of his arm, outside the room door nearly opposite my chair, encircling that maid's waist on the landing, like a table-cloth brush.

Therefore, I thought it just as well, before any London Philandering took place, that I should have a little time to look round me, and to see what girls were in and about the place. So, nobody stayed with me in my new lodging at first after Trottle had established me there safe and sound, but Peggy Flobbins, my maid; a most affectionate and attached woman, who never was an object of Philandering since I have known her, and is not likely to begin to become so after nine-and-twenty years next March.

It was the fifth of November when I first breakfasted in my new rooms. The Guys were going about in the brown fog, like

4

magnified monsters of insects in table-beer, and there was a Guy resting on the door-steps of the House to Let. I put on my glasses, partly to see how the boys were pleased with what I sent them out by Peggy, and partly to make sure that she didn't approach too near the ridiculous object, which of course was full of sky-rockets, and might go off into bangs at any moment. In this way it happened that the first time I ever looked at the House to Let, after I became its opposite neighbour, I had my glasses on. And this might not have happened once in fifty times, for my sight is uncommonly good for my time of life; and I wear glasses as little as I can, for fear of spoiling it.

I knew already that it was a ten-roomed house, very dirty, and much dilapidated; that the area-rails were rusty and peeling away, and that two or three of them were wanting, or half-wanting; that there were broken panes of glass in the windows, and blotches of mud on other panes, which the boys had thrown at them; that there was quite a collection of stones in the area, also proceeding from those Young Mischiefs; that there were games chalked on the pavement before the house, and likenesses of ghosts chalked on the street-door; that the windows were all darkened by rotting old blinds, or shutters, or both; that the bills "To Let," had curled up, as if the damp air of the place had given them cramps; or had dropped down into corners, as if they were no more. I had seen all this on my first visit, and I had remarked to Trottle, that the lower part of the black board about terms was split away; that the rest had become illegible, and that the very stone of the door-steps was broken across. Notwithstanding, I sat at my breakfast table on that Please to Remember the fifth of November morning, staring at the House through my glasses, as if I had never looked at it before.

All at once—in the first-floor window on my right—down in a low corner, at a hole in a blind or a shutter—I found that I was looking at a secret Eye. The reflection of my fire may have touched it and made it shine; but, I saw it shine and vanish.

The eye might have seen me, or it might not have seen me, sitting there in the glow of my fire—you can take which probability you prefer, without offence—but something struck through my frame, as if the sparkle of this eye had been electric, and had flashed straight at me. It had such an effect upon me, that I could not remain by myself, and I rang for Flobbins, and invented some little jobs for her, to keep her in the room. After my breakfast was cleared away, I sat in the same place with my glasses on, moving my head, now so, and now so, trying whether, with the shining of my fire and the flaws in the window-glass, I could reproduce any sparkle seeming to be up there, that was like the sparkle of an eye. But no; I could make nothing like it. I could make ripples and crooked lines in the front of the House to Let, and I could even twist one window up and loop it into another; but, I could make no eye, nor anything like an eye. So I convinced myself that I really had seen an eye.

Well, to be sure I could not get rid of the impression of this eye, and it troubled me and troubled me, until it was almost a torment. I don't think I was previously inclined to concern my head much about the opposite House; but, after this eye, my head was full of the house; and I thought of little else than the house, and I watched the house, and I talked about the house, and I dreamed of the house. In all this, I fully believe now, there was a good Providence. But, you will judge for yourself about that, bye-and-bye.

My landlord was a butler, who had married a cook, and set up housekeeping. They had not kept house longer than a couple of years, and they knew no more about the House to Let than I did. Neither could I find out anything concerning it among the trades-people or otherwise; further than what Trottle had told me at first. It had been empty, some said six years, some said eight, some said ten. It never did let, they all agreed, and it never would let.

6

I soon felt convinced that I should work myself into one of my states about the House; and I soon did. I lived for a whole month in a flurry, that was always getting worse. Towers's prescriptions, which I had brought to London with me, were of no more use than nothing. In the cold winter sunlight, in the thick winter fog, in the black winter rain, in the white winter snow, the House was equally on my mind. I have heard, as everybody else has, of a spirit's haunting a house; but I have had my own personal experience of a house's haunting a spirit; for that House haunted mine.

In all that month's time, I never saw anyone go into the House nor come out of the House. I supposed that such a thing must take place sometimes, in the dead of the night, or the glimmer of the morning; but, I never saw it done. I got no relief from having my curtains drawn when it came on dark, and shutting out the House. The Eye then began to shine in my fire.

I am a single old woman. I should say at once, without being at all afraid of the name, I am an old maid; only that I am older than the phrase would express. The time was when I had my love-trouble, but, it is long and long ago. He was killed at sea (Dear Heaven rest his blessed head!) when I was twenty-five. I have all my life, since ever I can remember, been deeply fond of children. I have always felt such a love for them, that I have had my sorrowful and sinful times when I have fancied something must have gone wrong in my life—something must have been turned aside from its original intention I mean—or I should have been the proud and happy mother of many children, and a fond old grandmother this day. I have soon known better in the cheerfulness and contentment that God has blessed me with and given me abundant reason for; and yet I have had to dry my eyes even then, when I have thought of my dear, brave, hopeful, handsome, bright-eyed Charley, and the trust meant to cheer me with. Charley was my youngest brother, and he went to India. He married there, and sent his gentle little wife home to

7

me to be confined, and she was to go back to him, and the baby was to be left with me, and I was to bring it up. It never belonged to this life. It took its silent place among the other incidents in my story that might have been, but never were. I had hardly time to whisper to her "Dead my own!" or she to answer, "Ashes to ashes, dust to dust! O lay it on my breast and comfort Charley!" when she had gone to seek her baby at Our Saviour's feet. I went to Charley, and I told him there was nothing left but me, poor me; and I lived with Charley, out there, several years. He was a man of fifty, when he fell asleep in my arms. His face had changed to be almost old and a little stern; but, it softened, and softened when I laid it down that I might cry and pray beside it; and, when I looked at it for the last time, it was my dear, untroubled, handsome, youthful Charley of long ago.

—I was going on to tell that the loneliness of the House to Let brought back all these recollections, and that they had quite pierced my heart one evening, when Flobbins, opening the door, and looking very much as if she wanted to laugh but thought better of it, said:

"Mr. Jabez Jarber, ma'am!"

Upon which Mr. Jarber ambled in, in his usual absurd way, saying:

"Sophonisba!"

Which I am obliged to confess is my name. A pretty one and proper one enough when it was given to me: but, a good many years out of date now, and always sounding particularly high-flown and comical from his lips. So I said, sharply:

"Though it is Sophonisba, Jarber, you are not obliged to mention it, that I see."

In reply to this observation, the ridiculous man put the tips of

8

my five right-hand fingers to his lips, and said again, with an aggravating accent on the third syllable:

"Sopho*ni*sba!"

I don't burn lamps, because I can't abide the smell of oil, and wax candles belonged to my day. I hope the convenient situation of one of my tall old candlesticks on the table at my elbow will be my excuse for saying, that if he did that again, I would chop his toes with it. (I am sorry to add that when I told him so, I knew his toes to be tender.) But, really, at my time of life and at Jarber's, it is too much of a good thing. There is an orchestra still standing in the open air at the Wells, before which, in the presence of a throng of fine company, I have walked a minuet with Jarber. But, there is a house still standing, in which I have worn a pinafore, and had a tooth drawn by fastening a thread to the tooth and the door-handle, and toddling away from the door. And how should I look now, at my years, in a pinafore, or having a door for my dentist?

Besides, Jarber always was more or less an absurd man. He was sweetly dressed, and beautifully perfumed, and many girls of my day would have given their ears for him; though I am bound to add that he never cared a fig for them, or their advances either, and that he was very constant to me. For, he not only proposed to me before my love-happiness ended in sorrow, but afterwards too: not once, nor yet twice: nor will we say how many times. However many they were, or however few they were, the last time he paid me that compliment was immediately after he had presented me with a digestive dinner-pill stuck on the point of a pin. And I said on that occasion, laughing heartily, "Now, Jarber, if you don't know that two people whose united ages would make about a hundred and fifty, have got to be old, I do; and I beg to swallow this nonsense in the form of this pill" (which I took on the spot), "and I request to, hear no more of it."

After that, he conducted himself pretty well. He was always a little squeezed man, was Jarber, in little sprigged waistcoats; and he had always little legs and a little smile, and a little voice, and little round-about ways. As long as I can remember him he was always going little errands for people, and carrying little gossip. At this present time when he called me "Sophonisba!" he had a little old-fashioned lodging in that new neighbourhood of mine. I had not seen him for two or three years, but I had heard that he still went out with a little perspective-glass and stood on door-steps in Saint James's Street, to see the nobility go to Court; and went in his little cloak and goloshes outside Willis's rooms to see them go to Almack's; and caught the frightfullest colds, and got himself trodden upon by coachmen and linkmen, until he went home to his landlady a mass of bruises, and had to be nursed for a month.

Jarber took off his little fur-collared cloak, and sat down opposite me, with his little cane and hat in his hand.

"Let us have no more Sophonisbaing, if *you* please, Jarber," I said. "Call me Sarah. How do you do? I hope you are pretty well."

"Thank you. And you?" said Jarber.

"I am as well as an old woman can expect to be."

Jarber was beginning:

"Say, not old, Sophon—" but I looked at the candlestick, and he left off; pretending not to have said anything.

"I am infirm, of course," I said, "and so are you. Let us both be thankful it's no worse."

"Is it possible that you look worried?" said Jarber.

"It is very possible. I have no doubt it is the fact."

"And what has worried my Soph-, soft-hearted friend," said Jarber.

10

"Something not easy, I suppose, to comprehend. I am worried to death by a House to Let, over the way."

Jarber went with his little tip-toe step to the window-curtains, peeped out, and looked round at me.

"Yes," said I, in answer: "that house."

After peeping out again, Jarber came back to his chair with a tender air, and asked: "How does it worry you, S-arah?"

"It is a mystery to me," said I. "Of course every house *is* a mystery, more or less; but, something that I don't care to mention" (for truly the Eye was so slight a thing to mention that I was more than half ashamed of it), "has made that House so mysterious to me, and has so fixed it in my mind, that I have had no peace for a month. I foresee that I shall have no peace, either, until Trottle comes to me, next Monday."

I might have mentioned before, that there is a lone-standing jealousy between Trottle and Jarber; and that there is never any love lost between those two.

"*Trottle,*" petulantly repeated Jarber, with a little flourish of his cane; "how is *Trottle* to restore the lost peace of Sarah?"

"He will exert himself to find out something about the House. I have fallen into that state about it, that I really must discover by some means or other, good or bad, fair or foul, how and why it is that that House remains To Let."

"And why Trottle? Why not," putting his little hat to his heart; "why not, Jarber?

"To tell you the truth, I have never thought of Jarber in the matter. And now I do think of Jarber, through your having the kindness to suggest him—for which I am really and truly obliged to you—I don't think he could do it."

11

"Sarah!"

"I think it would be too much for you, Jarber."

"Sarah!"

"There would be coming and going, and fetching and carrying, Jarber, and you might catch cold."

"Sarah! What can be done by Trottle, can be done by me. I am on terms of acquaintance with every person of responsibility in this parish. I am intimate at the Circulating Library. I converse daily with the Assessed Taxes. I lodge with the Water Rate. I know the Medical Man. I lounge habitually at the House Agent's. I dine with the Churchwardens. I move to the Guardians. Trottle! A person in the sphere of a domestic, and totally unknown to society!"

"Don't be warm, Jarber. In mentioning Trottle, I have naturally relied on my Right-Hand, who would take any trouble to gratify even a whim of his old mistress's. But, if you can find out anything to help to unravel the mystery of this House to Let, I shall be fully as much obliged to you as if there was never a Trottle in the land."

Jarber rose and put on his little cloak. A couple of fierce brass lions held it tight round his little throat; but a couple of the mildest Hares might have done that, I am sure. "Sarah," he said, "I go. Expect me on Monday evening, the Sixth, when perhaps you will give me a cup of tea;—may I ask for no Green? Adieu!"

This was on a Thursday, the second of December. When I reflected that Trottle would come back on Monday, too, I had my misgivings as to the difficulty of keeping the two powers from open warfare, and indeed I was more uneasy than I quite like to confess. However, the empty House swallowed up that thought next morning, as it swallowed up most other thoughts

12

now, and the House quite preyed upon me all that day, and all the Saturday.

It was a very wet Sunday: raining and blowing from morning to night. When the bells rang for afternoon church, they seemed to ring in the commotion of the puddles as well as in the wind, and they sounded very loud and dismal indeed, and the street looked very dismal indeed, and the House looked dismallest of all.

I was reading my prayers near the light, and my fire was growing in the darkening window-glass, when, looking up, as I prayed for the fatherless children and widows and all who were desolate and oppressed,—I saw the Eye again. It passed in a moment, as it had done before; but, this time, I was inwardly more convinced that I had seen it.

Well to be sure, I *had* a night that night! Whenever I closed my own eyes, it was to see eyes. Next morning, at an unreasonably, and I should have said (but for that railroad) an impossibly early hour, comes Trottle. As soon as he had told me all about the Wells, I told him all about the House. He listened with as great interest and attention as I could possibly wish, until I came to Jabez Jarber, when he cooled in an instant, and became opinionated.

"Now, Trottle," I said, pretending not to notice, "when Mr. Jarber comes back this evening, we must all lay our heads together."

"I should hardly think that would be wanted, ma'am; Mr. Jarber's head is surely equal to anything."

Being determined not to notice, I said again, that we must all lay our heads together.

"Whatever you order, ma'am, shall be obeyed. Still, it cannot be

13

doubted, I should think, that Mr. Jarber's head is equal, if not superior, to any pressure that can be brought to bear upon it."

This was provoking; and his way, when he came in and out all through the day, of pretending not to see the House to Let, was more provoking still. However, being quite resolved not to notice, I gave no sign whatever that I did notice. But, when evening came, and he showed in Jarber, and, when Jarber wouldn't be helped off with his cloak, and poked his cane into cane chair-backs and china ornaments and his own eye, in trying to unclasp his brazen lions of himself (which he couldn't do, after all), I could have shaken them both.

As it was, I only shook the tea-pot, and made the tea. Jarber had brought from under his cloak, a roll of paper, with which he had triumphantly pointed over the way, like the Ghost of Hamlet's Father appearing to the late Mr. Kemble, and which he had laid on the table.

"A discovery?" said I, pointing to it, when he was seated, and had got his tea-cup.—"Don't go, Trottle."

"The first of a series of discoveries," answered Jarber. "Account of a former tenant, compiled from the Water Rate, and Medical Man."

"Don't go, Trottle," I repeated. For, I saw him making imperceptibly to the door.

"Begging your pardon, ma'am, I might be in Mr. Jarber's way?"

Jarber looked that he decidedly thought he might be. I relieved myself with a good angry croak, and said—always determined not to notice:

"Have the goodness to sit down, if you please, Trottle. I wish you to hear this."

Trottle bowed in the stiffest manner, and took the remotest chair

14

he could find. Even that, he moved close to the draught from the keyhole of the door.

"Firstly," Jarber began, after sipping his tea, "would my Sophon—"

"Begin again, Jarber," said I.

"Would you be much surprised, if this House to Let should turn out to be the property of a relation of your own?"

"I should indeed be very much surprised."

"Then it belongs to your first cousin (I learn, by the way, that he is ill at this time) George Forley."

"Then that is a bad beginning. I cannot deny that George Forley stands in the relation of first cousin to me; but I hold no communication with him. George Forley has been a hard, bitter, stony father to a child now dead. George Forley was most implacable and unrelenting to one of his two daughters who made a poor marriage. George Forley brought all the weight of his band to bear as heavily against that crushed thing, as he brought it to bear lightly, favouringly, and advantageously upon her sister, who made a rich marriage. I hope that, with the measure George Forley meted, it may not be measured out to him again. I will give George Forley no worse wish."

I was strong upon the subject, and I could not keep the tears out of my eyes; for, that young girl's was a cruel story, and I had dropped many a tear over it before.

"The house being George Forley's," said I, "is almost enough to account for there being a Fate upon it, if Fate there is. Is there anything about George Forley in those sheets of paper?"

"Not a word."

"I am glad to hear it. Please to read on. Trottle, why don't you

15

come nearer? Why do you sit mortifying yourself in those arctic regions? Come nearer."

"Thank you, ma'am; I am quite near enough to Mr. Jarber."

Jarber rounded his chair, to get his back full to my opinionated friend and servant, and, beginning to read, tossed the words at him over his (Jabez Jarber's) own ear and shoulder.

He read what follows:

THE MANCHESTER MARRIAGE

Mr. and Mrs. Openshaw came from Manchester to London and took the House To Let. He had been, what is called in Lancashire, a Salesman for a large manufacturing firm, who were extending their business, and opening a warehouse in London; where Mr. Openshaw was now to superintend the business. He rather enjoyed the change of residence; having a kind of curiosity about London, which he had never yet been able to gratify in his brief visits to the metropolis. At the same time he had an odd, shrewd, contempt for the inhabitants; whom he had always pictured to himself as fine, lazy people; caring nothing but for fashion and aristocracy, and lounging away their days in Bond Street, and such places; ruining good English, and ready in their turn to despise him as a provincial. The hours that the men of business kept in the city scandalised him too; accustomed as he was to the early dinners of Manchester folk, and the consequently far longer evenings. Still, he was pleased to go to London; though he would not for the world have confessed it, even to himself, and always spoke of the step to his friends as one demanded of him by the interests of his employers, and sweetened to him by a considerable increase of salary. His salary indeed was so liberal that he might have been justified in taking a much larger House than this one, had he not thought himself bound to set an example to Londoners of how little a Manchester man of business cared for show. Inside, however, he furnished the House with an unusual degree of comfort, and, in the winter time, he insisted on keeping up as large fires as the grates would allow, in every room where the temperature was in the least chilly. Moreover, his northern sense of hospitality was such, that, if he were at home, he could hardly suffer a visitor to leave the house without forcing meat and drink upon him. Every servant in the house was well warmed, well fed, and kindly treated; for their master scorned all petty saving in aught that conduced to comfort; while he amused himself by following out all his accustomed habits and individual ways in defiance of what any of his new neighbours might think.

His wife was a pretty, gentle woman, of suitable age and character. He was forty-two, she thirty-five. He was loud and decided; she soft and yielding. They had two children or rather, I should say, she had two; for the elder, a girl of eleven, was Mrs. Openshaw's child by Frank Wilson her first husband. The younger was a little boy, Edwin, who could just prattle, and to whom his father delighted to speak in the broadest and most unintelligible Lancashire dialect, in order to keep up what he called the true Saxon accent.

Mrs. Openshaw's Christian-name was Alice, and her first husband had been her own cousin. She was the orphan niece of a sea-captain in Liverpool: a quiet, grave little creature, of great personal attraction when she was fifteen or sixteen, with regular features and a blooming complexion. But she was very shy, and believed herself to be very stupid and awkward; and was frequently scolded by her aunt, her own uncle's second wife. So when her cousin, Frank Wilson, came home from a long absence at sea, and first was kind and protective to her; secondly, attentive and thirdly, desperately in love with her, she hardly knew how to be grateful enough to him. It is true she would have preferred his remaining in the first or second stages of behaviour; for his violent love puzzled and frightened her. Her uncle neither helped nor hindered the love affair though it was going on under his own eyes. Frank's step-mother had such a variable temper, that there was no knowing whether what she liked one day she would like the next, or not. At length she went to such extremes of crossness, that Alice was only too glad to shut her eyes and rush blindly at the chance of escape from domestic tyranny offered her by a marriage with her cousin;

and, liking him better than any one in the world except her uncle (who was at this time at sea) she went off one morning and was married to him; her only bridesmaid being the housemaid at her aunt's. The consequence was, that Frank and his wife went into lodgings, and Mrs. Wilson refused to see them, and turned away Norah, the warm-hearted housemaid; whom they accordingly took into their service. When Captain Wilson returned from his voyage, he was very cordial with the young couple, and spent many an evening at their lodgings; smoking his pipe, and sipping his grog; but he told them that, for quietness' sake, he could not ask them to his own house; for his wife was bitter against them. They were not very unhappy about this.

The seed of future unhappiness lay rather in Frank's vehement, passionate disposition; which led him to resent his wife's shyness and want of demonstration as failures in conjugal duty. He was already tormenting himself, and her too, in a slighter degree, by apprehensions and imaginations of what might befall her during his approaching absence at sea. At last he went to his father and urged him to insist upon Alice's being once more received under his roof; the more especially as there was now a prospect of her confinement while her husband was away on his voyage. Captain Wilson was, as he himself expressed it, "breaking up," and unwilling to undergo the excitement of a scene; yet he felt that what his son said was true. So he went to his wife. And before Frank went to sea, he had the comfort of seeing his wife installed in her old little garret in his father's house. To have placed her in the one best spare room was a step beyond Mrs. Wilson's powers of submission or generosity. The worst part about it, however, was that the faithful Norah had to be dismissed. Her place as housemaid had been filled up; and, even had it not, she had forfeited Mrs. Wilson's good opinion for ever. She comforted her young master and mistress by pleasant prophecies of the time when they would have a household of their own; of which, in whatever service she might be in the meantime, she should be sure to form part. Almost the last action Frank Wilson did, before setting sail, was going with Alice to see Norah once more at her mother's house. And then he went away.

Alice's father-in-law grew more and more feeble as winter advanced. She was of great use to her step-mother in nursing and amusing him; and, although there was anxiety enough in the household, there was perhaps more of peace than there had been for years; for Mrs. Wilson had not a bad heart, and was softened by the visible approach of death to one whom she loved, and touched by the lonely condition of the young creature, expecting her first confinement in her husband's absence. To this relenting mood Norah owed the permission to come and nurse Alice when her baby was born, and to remain to attend on Captain Wilson.

Before one letter had been received from Frank (who had sailed for the East Indies and China), his father died. Alice was always glad to remember that he had held her baby in his arms, and kissed and blessed it before his death. After that, and the consequent examination into the state of his affairs, it was found that he had left far less property than people had been led by his style of living to imagine; and, what money there was, was all settled upon his wife, and at her disposal after her death. This did not signify much to Alice, as Frank was now first mate of his ship, and, in another voyage or two, would be captain. Meanwhile he had left her some hundreds (all his savings) in the bank.

It became time for Alice to hear from her husband. One letter from the Cape she had already received. The next was to announce his arrival in India. As week after week passed over, and no intelligence of the ship's arrival reached the office of the owners, and the Captain's wife was in the same state of ignorant suspense as Alice herself, her fears grew most oppressive. At length the day came when, in reply to her inquiry at the Shipping Office, they told her that the owners had given up Hope of ever hearing more of the Betsy-Jane, and had sent in their claim upon the underwriters. Now that he was gone for ever, she first felt a yearning, longing love for the kind cousin, the dear friend, the sympathising protector, whom she should never see again,—first felt a passionate desire to show him his child, whom she had hitherto rather craved to have all to herself—her own sole possession. Her grief was, however, noiseless, and quiet—rather to the scandal of Mrs. Wilson; who bewailed her step-son as if he and she had always lived together in perfect harmony, and who evidently thought it her duty to burst into fresh tears at every strange face she saw; dwelling on his poor young widow's desolate state, and the helplessness of the fatherless child, with an unction, as if she liked the excitement of the sorrowful story.

So passed away the first days of Alice's widowhood. Bye-and-bye things subsided into their natural and tranquil course. But, as if this young creature was always to be in some heavy trouble, her ewe-lamb began to be ailing, pining and sickly. The child's mysterious illness turned out to be some affection of the spine likely to affect health; but not to shorten life—at least so the doctors said. But the long dreary suffering of one whom a mother loves as Alice loved her only child, is hard to look forward to. Only Norah guessed what Alice suffered; no one but God knew.

And so it fell out, that when Mrs. Wilson, the elder, came to her one day in violent distress, occasioned by a very material diminution in the value the property that her husband had left her,—a diminution which made her income barely enough to support herself, much less Alice—the latter could hardly understand how anything which did not touch health or life could cause such grief; and she received the intelligence with irritating composure. But when, that afternoon, the little sick child was brought in, and the grandmother—who after all loved it well—began a fresh moan over her losses to its unconscious ears—saying how she had planned to consult this or that doctor, and to give it this or that comfort or luxury in after yearn but that now all chance of this had passed away—Alice's heart was touched, and she drew near to Mrs. Wilson with unwonted caresses, and, in a spirit not unlike to that of, Ruth, entreated, that come what would, they might remain together. After much discussion in succeeding days, it was arranged that Mrs. Wilson should take a house in Manchester, furnishing it partly with what furniture she had, and providing the rest with Alice's remaining two hundred pounds. Mrs. Wilson was herself a Manchester woman, and naturally longed to return to her native town. Some connections of her own at that time required lodgings, for which they were willing to pay pretty handsomely. Alice undertook the active superintendence and superior work of the household. Norah, willing faithful Norah, offered to cook, scour, do anything in short, so that, she might but remain with them.

The plan succeeded. For some years their first lodgers remained with them, and all went smoothly,—with the one sad exception of the little girl's increasing deformity. How that mother loved that child, is not for words to tell!

Then came a break of misfortune. Their lodgers left, and no one succeeded to them. After some months they had to remove to a smaller house; and Alice's tender conscience was torn by the idea that she ought not to be a burden to her mother-in-law, but ought to go out and seek her own maintenance. And leave her child! The thought came like the sweeping boom of a funeral bell over her heart.

Bye-and-bye, Mr. Openshaw came to lodge with them. He had started in life as the errand-boy and sweeper-out of a warehouse; had struggled up through all the grades of employment in the place, fighting his way through the hard striving Manchester life with strong pushing energy of character. Every spare moment of time had been sternly given up to self-teaching. He was a capital accountant, a good French and German scholar, a keen, far-seeing tradesman; understanding markets, and the bearing of events, both near and distant, on trade: and yet, with such vivid attention to present details, that I do not think he ever saw a group of flowers in the fields without thinking whether their colours would, or would not, form harmonious contrasts in the coming spring muslins and prints. He went to debating societies, and threw himself with all his heart and soul into politics; esteeming, it must be owned, every man a fool or a knave who differed from him, and overthrowing his opponents rather by the loud strength of his language than the calm strength if his logic. There was something of the Yankee in all this. Indeed his theory ran parallel to the famous Yankee motto—"England flogs creation, and Manchester flogs England." Such a man, as may be fancied, had had no time for falling in love, or any such nonsense. At the age when most young men go through their courting and matrimony, he had not the means of keeping a wife, and was far too practical to think of having one. And now that he was in easy circumstances, a rising man, he considered women almost as incumbrances to the world, with whom a man had better have as little to do as possible. His first impression of Alice was indistinct, and he did not care enough about her to make it distinct. "A pretty yea-nay kind of woman," would have been his description of her, if he had been pushed into a corner. He was rather afraid, in the beginning, that her quiet ways arose from a listlessness and laziness of character which would have been exceedingly discordant to his active energetic nature. But, when he found out the punctuality with which his wishes were attended to, and her work was done; when he was called in the morning at the very stroke of the clock, his shaving-water scalding hot, his fire bright, his coffee made exactly as his peculiar fancy dictated, (for he was a man who had his theory about everything, based upon what he knew of science, and often perfectly original)—then he began to think: not that Alice had any peculiar merit; but that he had got into remarkably good lodgings: his restlessness wore away, and he began to consider himself as almost settled for life in them.

Mr. Openshaw had been too busy, all his life, to be introspective. He did not know that he had any tenderness in his nature; and if he had become conscious of its abstract existence, he would have considered it as a manifestation of disease in some part of his nature. But he was decoyed into pity unawares; and pity led on to tenderness. That little helpless child—always carried about by one of the three busy women of the house, or else patiently threading coloured beads in the chair from which, by no effort of its own, could it ever move; the great grave blue eyes, full of serious, not uncheerful, expression, giving to the small delicate face a look beyond its years; the soft plaintive voice dropping out but few words, so unlike the continual prattle of a child—caught Mr. Openshaw's attention in spite of himself. One day—he half scorned himself for doing so—he cut short his dinner-hour to go in search of some toy which should take the place of those eternal beads. I forget what he bought; but, when he gave the present (which he took care to do in a short abrupt manner, and when no one was by to see him) he was almost thrilled by the flash of delight that came over that child's face, and could not help all through that afternoon going over and over again the picture left on his memory, by the bright effect of unexpected joy on the little girl's face. When he returned home, he found his slippers placed by his sitting-room fire; and even more careful attention paid to his fancies than was habitual in those model lodgings. When Alice had taken the last of his tea-things away—she had been silent as usual till then—she stood for an instant with the door in her hand. Mr. Openshaw looked as if he were deep in his book, though in fact he did not see a line; but was heartily wishing the woman would be gone, and not make any palaver of gratitude. But she only said:

"I am very much obliged to you, sir. Thank you very much," and was gone, even before he could send her away with a "There, my good woman, that's enough!"

For some time longer he took no apparent notice of the child. He even hardened his heart into disregarding her sudden flush of colour, and little timid smile of recognition, when he saw her by chance. But, after all, this could not last for ever; and, having a second time given way to tenderness, there was no relapse. The insidious enemy having thus entered his heart, in the guise of compassion to the child, soon assumed the more dangerous form of interest in the mother. He was aware of this change of feeling, despised himself for it, struggled with it nay, internally yielded to it and cherished it, long before he suffered the slightest expression of it, by word, action, or look, to escape him. He watched Alice's docile obedient ways to her stepmother; the love which she had inspired in the rough Norah (roughened by the wear and tear of sorrow and years); but above all, he saw the wild, deep, passionate affection existing between her and her child. They spoke little to any one else, or when any one else was by; but, when alone together, they talked, and murmured, and cooed, and chattered so continually, that Mr. Openshaw first wondered what they could find to say to each other, and next became irritated because they were always so grave and silent with him. All this time, he was perpetually devising small new pleasures for the child. His thoughts ran, in a pertinacious way, upon the desolate life before her; and often he came back from his day's work loaded with the very thing Alice had been longing for, but had not been able to procure. One time it was a little chair for drawing the little sufferer along the streets, and many an evening that ensuing summer Mr. Openshaw drew her along himself, regardless of the remarks of his acquaintances. One day in autumn he put down his newspaper, as Alice came in with the breakfast, and said, in as indifferent a voice as he could assume:

"Mrs. Frank, is there any reason why we two should not put up our horses together?"

Alice stood still in perplexed wonder. What did he mean? He had resumed the reading of his newspaper, as if he did not expect any answer; so she found silence her safest course, and went on quietly arranging his breakfast without another word passing between them. Just as he was leaving the house, to go to the warehouse as usual, he turned back and put his head into the bright, neat, tidy kitchen, where all the women breakfasted in the morning:

"You'll think of what I said, Mrs. Frank" (this was her name with the lodgers), "and let me have your opinion upon it to-night."

Alice was thankful that her mother and Norah were too busy talking together to attend much to this speech. She determined not to think about it at all through the day; and, of course, the effort not to think made her think all the more. At night she sent up Norah with his tea. But Mr. Openshaw almost knocked Norah down as she was going out at the door, by pushing past her and calling out "Mrs. Frank!" in an impatient voice, at the top of the stairs.

Alice went up, rather than seem to have affixed too much meaning to his words.

"Well, Mrs. Frank," he said, "what answer? Don't make it too long; for I have lots of office-work to get through to-night."

"I hardly know what you meant, sir," said truthful Alice.

"Well! I should have thought you might have guessed. You're not new at this sort of work, and I am. However, I'll make it plain this time. Will you have me to be thy wedded husband, and serve me, and love me, and honour me, and all that sort of thing? Because if you will, I will do as much by you, and be a father to your child—and that's more than is put in the prayer-book. Now, I'm a man of my word; and what I say, I feel; and what I promise, I'll do. Now, for your answer!"

Alice was silent. He began to make the tea, as if her reply was a matter of perfect indifference to him; but, as soon as that was done, he became impatient.

"Well?" said he.

"How long, sir, may I have to think over it?"

"Three minutes!" (looking at his watch). "You've had two already—that makes five. Be a sensible woman, say Yes, and sit down to tea with me, and we'll talk it over together; for, after tea, I shall be busy; say No" (he hesitated a moment to try and keep his voice in the same tone), "and I shan't say another word about it, but pay up a year's rent for my rooms to-morrow, and be off. Time's up! Yes or no?"

"If you please, sir,—you have been so good to little Ailsie—"

"There, sit down comfortably by me on the sofa, and let us have our tea together. I am glad to find you are as good and sensible as I took for."

And this was Alice Wilson's second wooing.

Mr. Openshaw's will was too strong, and his circumstances too good, for him not to carry all before him. He settled Mrs. Wilson in a comfortable house of her own, and made her quite independent of lodgers. The little that Alice said with regard to future plans was in Norah's behalf.

"No," said Mr. Openshaw. "Norah shall take care of the old lady as long as she lives; and, after that, she shall either come and live with us, or, if she likes it better, she shall have a provision for life—for your sake, missus. No one who has been good to you or the child shall go unrewarded. But even the little one will be better for some fresh stuff about her. Get her a bright, sensible girl as a nurse: one who won't go rubbing her with calf's-foot jelly as Norah does; wasting good stuff outside that ought to go in, but will follow doctors' directions; which, as you must see pretty clearly by this time, Norah won't; because they give the poor little wench pain. Now, I'm not above being nesh for other folks myself. I can stand a good blow, and never change colour; but, set me in the operating-room in the infirmary, and I turn as sick as a girl. Yet, if need were, I would hold the little wench on my knees while she screeched with pain, if it were to do her poor back good. Nay, nay, wench! keep your white looks for the time when it comes—I don't say it ever will. But this I know, Norah will spare the child and cheat the doctor if she can. Now, I say, give the bairn a year or two's chance, and then, when the pack of doctors have done their best—and, maybe, the old lady has gone—we'll have Norah back, or do better for her."

The pack of doctors could do no good to little Ailsie. She was beyond their power. But her father (for so he insisted on being called, and also on Alice's no longer retaining the appellation of Mama, but becoming henceforward Mother), by his healthy cheerfulness of manner, his clear decision of purpose, his odd turns and quirks of humour, added to his real strong love for the helpless little girl, infused a new element of brightness and confidence into her life; and, though her back remained the same, her general health was strengthened, and Alice—never going beyond a smile herself—had the pleasure of seeing her child taught to laugh.

As for Alice's own life, it was happier than it had ever been. Mr. Openshaw required no demonstration, no expressions of affection from her. Indeed, these would rather have disgusted him. Alice could love deeply, but could not talk about it. The perpetual requirement of loving words, looks, and caresses, and misconstruing their absence into absence of love, had been the great trial of her former married life. Now, all went on clear and straight, under the guidance of her husband's strong sense, warm heart, and powerful will. Year by year their worldly prosperity increased. At Mrs. Wilson's death, Norah came back to them, as nurse to the newly-born little Edwin; into which post she was not installed without a pretty strong oration on the part of the proud and happy father; who declared that if he found out that Norah ever tried to screen the boy by a falsehood, or to make him nesh either in body or mind, she should go that very day. Norah and Mr. Openshaw were not on the most thoroughly cordial terms; neither of them fully recognising or appreciating the other's best qualities.

This was the previous history of the Lancashire family who had now removed to London, and had come to occupy the House.

They had been there about a year, when Mr. Openshaw suddenly informed his wife that he had determined to heal long-standing feuds, and had asked his uncle and aunt Chadwick to come and pay them a visit and see London. Mrs. Openshaw had never seen this uncle and aunt of her husband's. Years before she had married him, there had been a quarrel. All she knew was, that Mr. Chadwick was a small manufacturer in a country town in South Lancashire. She was extremely pleased that the breach was to be healed, and began making preparations to render their visit pleasant.

They arrived at last. Going to see London was such an event to them, that Mrs. Chadwick had made all new linen fresh for the occasion-from night-caps downwards; and, as for gowns, ribbons, and collars, she might have been going into the wilds of Canada where never a shop is, so large was her stock. A fortnight before the day of her departure for London, she had formally called to take leave of all her acquaintance; saying she should need all the intermediate time for packing up. It was like a second wedding in her imagination; and, to complete the resemblance which an entirely new wardrobe made between the two events, her husband brought her back from Manchester, on the last market-day before they set off, a gorgeous pearl and amethyst brooch, saying, "Lunnon should see that Lancashire folks knew a handsome thing when they saw it."

For some time after Mr. and Mrs. Chadwick arrived at the Openshaws', there was no opportunity for wearing this brooch; but at length they obtained an order to see Buckingham Palace, and the spirit of loyalty demanded that Mrs. Chadwick should wear her best clothes in visiting the abode of her sovereign. On her return, she hastily changed her dress; for Mr. Openshaw had planned that they should go to Richmond, drink tea and return by moonlight. Accordingly, about five o'clock, Mr. and Mrs. Openshaw and Mr. and Mrs. Chadwick set off.

The housemaid and cook sate below, Norah hardly knew where. She was always engrossed in the nursery, in tending her two children, and in sitting by the restless, excitable Ailsie till she fell asleep. Bye-and-bye, the housemaid Bessy tapped gently at the door. Norah went to her, and they spoke in whispers.

"Nurse! there's some one down-stairs wants you."

"Wants me! Who is it?"

"A gentleman—"

"A gentleman? Nonsense!"

"Well! a man, then, and he asks for you, and he rung at the front door bell, and has walked into the dining-room."

"You should never have let him," exclaimed Norah, "master and missus out—"

"I did not want him to come in; but when he heard you lived here, he walked past me, and sat down on the first chair, and said, 'Tell her to come and speak to me.' There is no gas lighted in the room, and supper is all set out."

"He'll be off with the spoons!" exclaimed Norah, putting the housemaid's fear into words, and preparing to leave the room, first, however, giving a look to Ailsie, sleeping soundly and calmly.

Down-stairs she went, uneasy fears stirring in her bosom. Before she entered the dining-room she provided herself with a candle, and, with it in her hand, she went in, looking round her in the darkness for her visitor.

He was standing up, holding by the table. Norah and he looked at each other; gradual recognition coming into their eyes.

"Norah?" at length he asked.

"Who are you?" asked Norah, with the sharp tones of alarm and incredulity. "I don't know you:" trying, by futile words of disbelief, to do away with the terrible fact before her.

"Am I so changed?" he said, pathetically. "I daresay I am. But, Norah, tell me!" he breathed hard, "where is my wife? Is she—is she alive?"

He came nearer to Norah, and would have taken her hand; but she backed away from him; looking at him all the time with staring eyes, as if he were some horrible object. Yet he was a handsome, bronzed, good-looking fellow, with beard and moustache, giving him a foreign-looking aspect; but his eyes! there was no mistaking those eager, beautiful eyes—the very same that Norah had watched not half-an-hour ago, till sleep stole softly over them.

"Tell me, Norah—I can bear it—I have feared it so often. Is she dead?" Norah still kept silence. "She is dead!" He hung on Norah's words and looks, as if for confirmation or contradiction.

"What shall I do?" groaned Norah. "O, sir! why did you come? how did you find me out? where have you been? We thought you dead, we did, indeed!" She poured out words and questions to gain time, as if time would help her.

"Norah! answer me this question, straight, by yes or no—Is my wife dead?"

"No, she is not!" said Norah, slowly and heavily.

"O what a relief! Did she receive my letters? But perhaps you don't know. Why did you leave her? Where is she? O Norah, tell me all quickly!"

"Mr. Frank!" said Norah at last, almost driven to bay by her terror lest her mistress should return at any moment, and find him there—unable to consider what was best to be done or said—rushing at something decisive, because she could not endure her present state: "Mr. Frank! we never heard a line from you, and the shipowners said you had gone down, you and every one else. We thought you were dead, if ever man was, and poor Miss Alice and her little sick, helpless child! O, sir, you must guess it," cried the poor creature at last, bursting out into a passionate fit of crying, "for indeed I cannot tell it. But it was no one's fault. God help us all this night!"

Norah had sate down. She trembled too much to stand. He took her hands in his. He squeezed them hard, as if by physical pressure, the truth could be wrung out.

"Norah!" This time his tone was calm, stagnant as despair. "She has married again!"

Norah shook her head sadly. The grasp slowly relaxed. The man had fainted.

There was brandy in the room. Norah forced some drops into Mr. Frank's mouth, chafed his hands, and—when mere animal life returned, before the mind poured in its flood of memories and thoughts—she lifted him up, and rested his head against her knees. Then she put a few crumbs of bread taken from the supper-table, soaked in brandy into his mouth. Suddenly he sprang to his feet.

"Where is she? Tell me this instant." He looked so wild, so mad, so desperate, that Norah felt herself to be in bodily danger; but her time of dread had gone by. She had been afraid to tell him the truth, and then she had been a coward. Now, her wits were sharpened by the sense of his desperate state. He must leave the house. She would pity him afterwards; but now she must rather command and upbraid; for he must leave the house before her mistress came home. That one necessity stood clear before her.

"She is not here; that is enough for you to know. Nor can I say exactly where she is" (which was true to the letter if not to the spirit). "Go away, and tell me where to find you to-morrow, and I will tell you all. My master and mistress may come back at any minute, and then what would become of me with a strange man in the house?"

Such an argument was too petty to touch his excited mind.

"I don't care for your master and mistress. If your master is a man, he must feel for me poor shipwrecked sailor that I am—kept for years a prisoner amongst savages, always, always, always thinking of my wife and my home—dreaming of her by night, talking to her, though she could not hear, by day. I loved her more than all heaven and earth put together. Tell me where she is, this instant, you wretched woman, who salved over her wickedness to her, as you do to me."

The clock struck ten. Desperate positions require desperate measures.

33

"If you will leave the house now, I will come to you to-morrow and tell you all. What is more, you shall see your child now. She lies sleeping up-stairs. O, sir, you have a child, you do not know that as yet—a little weakly girl—with just a heart and soul beyond her years. We have reared her up with such care: We watched her, for we thought for many a year she might die any day, and we tended her, and no hard thing has come near her, and no rough word has ever been said to her. And now you, come and will take her life into your hand, and will crush it. Strangers to her have been kind to her; but her own father— Mr. Frank, I am her nurse, and I love her, and I tend her, and I would do anything for her that I could. Her mother's heart beats as hers beats; and, if she suffers a pain, her mother trembles all over. If she is happy, it is her mother that smiles and is glad. If she is growing stronger, her mother is healthy: if she dwindles, her mother languishes. If she dies—well, I don't know: it is not every one can lie down and die when they wish it. Come up-stairs, Mr. Frank, and see your child. Seeing her will do good to your poor heart. Then go away, in God's name, just this one night-to-morrow, if need be, you can do anything—kill us all if you will, or show yourself—a great grand man, whom God will bless for ever and ever. Come, Mr. Frank, the look of a sleeping child is sure to give peace."

She led him up-stairs; at first almost helping his steps, till they came near the nursery door. She had almost forgotten the existence of little Edwin. It struck upon her with affright as the shaded light fell upon the other cot; but she skilfully threw that corner of the room into darkness, and let the light fall on the sleeping Ailsie. The child had thrown down the coverings, and her deformity, as she lay with her back to them, was plainly visible through her slight night-gown. Her little face, deprived of the lustre of her eyes, looked wan and pinched, and had a pathetic expression in it, even as she slept. The poor father looked and looked with hungry, wistful eyes, into which the big tears came swelling up slowly, and dropped heavily down, as he stood trembling and shaking all over. Norah was angry with herself for growing impatient of the length of time that long lingering gaze lasted. She thought that she waited for full half-an-hour before Frank stirred. And then—instead of going away—he sank down on his knees by the bedside, and buried his face in the clothes. Little Ailsie stirred uneasily. Norah pulled him up in terror. She could afford no more time even for prayer in her extremity of fear; for surely the next moment would bring her mistress home. She took him forcibly by the arm; but, as he was going, his eye lighted on the other bed: he stopped. Intelligence came back into his face. His hands clenched.

"His child?" he asked.

"Her child," replied Norah. "God watches over him," said she instinctively; for Frank's looks excited her fears, and she needed to remind herself of the Protector of the helpless.

"God has not watched over me," he said, in despair; his thoughts apparently recoiling on his own desolate, deserted state. But Norah had no time for pity. To-morrow she would be as compassionate as her heart prompted. At length she guided him downstairs and shut the outer door and bolted it—as if by bolts to keep out facts.

Then she went back into the dining-room and effaced all traces of his presence as far as she could. She went upstairs to the nursery and sate there, her head on her hand, thinking what was to come of all this misery. It seemed to her very long before they did return; yet it was hardly eleven o'clock. She so heard the loud, hearty Lancashire voices on the stairs; and, for the first time, she understood the contrast of the desolation of the poor man who had so lately gone forth in lonely despair.

It almost put her out of patience to see Mrs. Openshaw come in, calmly smiling, handsomely dressed, happy, easy, to inquire after her children.

"Did Ailsie go to sleep comfortably?" she whispered to Norah.

"Yes."

Her mother bent over her, looking at her slumbers with the soft eyes of love. How little she dreamed who had looked on her last! Then she went to Edwin, with perhaps less wistful anxiety in her countenance, but more of pride. She took off her things, to go down to supper. Norah saw her no more that night.

Beside the door into the passage, the sleeping-nursery opened out of Mr. and Mrs. Openshaw's room, in order that they might have the children more immediately under their own eyes. Early the next summer morning Mrs. Openshaw was awakened by Ailsie's startled call of "Mother! mother!" She sprang up, put on her dressing-gown, and went to her child. Ailsie was only half awake, and in a not uncommon state of terror.

"Who was he, mother? Tell me!"

"Who, my darling? No one is here. You have been dreaming love. Waken up quite. See, it is broad daylight."

"Yes," said Ailsie, looking round her; then clinging to her mother, said, "but a man was here in the night, mother."

"Nonsense, little goose. No man has ever come near you!"

"Yes, he did. He stood there. Just by Norah. A man with hair and a beard. And he knelt down and said his prayers. Norah knows he was here, mother" (half angrily, as Mrs. Openshaw shook her head in smiling incredulity).

"Well! we will ask Norah when she comes," said Mrs. Openshaw, soothingly. "But we won't talk any more about him now. It is not five o'clock; it is too early for you to get up. Shall I fetch you a book and read to you?"

"Don't leave me, mother," said the child, clinging to her. So Mrs. Openshaw sate on the bedside talking to Ailsie, and telling her of what they had done at Richmond the evening before, until the little girl's eyes slowly closed and she once more fell asleep.

"What was the matter?" asked Mr. Openshaw, as his wife returned to bed. "Ailsie wakened up in a fright, with some story of a man having been in the room to say his prayers, — a dream, I suppose." And no more was said at the time.

Mrs. Openshaw had almost forgotten the whole affair when she got up about seven o'clock. But, bye-and-bye, she heard a sharp altercation going on in the nursery. Norah speaking angrily to Ailsie, a most unusual thing. Both Mr. and Mrs. Openshaw listened in astonishment.

"Hold your tongue, Ailsie; let me hear none of your dreams; never let me hear you tell that story again!" Ailsie began to cry.

Mr. Openshaw opened the door of communication before his wife could say a word.

"Norah, come here!"

The nurse stood at the door, defiant. She perceived she had been heard, but she was desperate.

"Don't let me hear you speak in that manner to Ailsie again," he said sternly, and shut the door.

Norah was infinitely relieved; for she had dreaded some questioning; and a little blame for sharp speaking was what she could well bear, if cross-examination was let alone.

Down-stairs they went, Mr. Openshaw carrying Ailsie; the sturdy Edwin coming step by step, right foot foremost, always holding his mother's hand. Each child was placed in a chair by the breakfast-table, and then Mr. and Mrs. Openshaw stood together at the window, awaiting their visitors' appearance and making plans for the day. There was a pause. Suddenly Mr. Openshaw turned to Ailsie, and said:

"What a little goosy somebody is with her dreams, waking up poor, tired mother in the middle of the night with a story of a man being in the room."

"Father! I'm sure I saw him," said Ailsie, half crying. "I don't want to make Norah angry; but I was not asleep, for all she says I was. I had been asleep,—and I awakened up quite wide awake though I was so frightened. I kept my eyes nearly shut, and I saw the man quite plain. A great brown man with a beard. He said his prayers. And then he looked at Edwin. And then Norah took him by the arm and led him away, after they had whispered a bit together."

"Now, my little woman must be reasonable," said Mr. Openshaw, who was always patient with Ailsie. "There was no man in the house last night at all. No man comes into the house as you know, if you think; much less goes up into the nursery. But sometimes we dream something has happened, and the dream is so like reality, that you are not the first person, little woman, who has stood out that the thing has really happened."

"But, indeed it was not a dream!" said Ailsie, beginning to cry.

Just then Mr. and Mrs. Chadwick came down, looking grave and discomposed. All during breakfast time they were silent and uncomfortable. As soon as the breakfast things were taken away, and the children had been carried up-stairs, Mr. Chadwick began in an evidently preconcerted manner to inquire if his nephew was certain that all his servants were honest; for, that Mrs. Chadwick had that morning missed a very valuable

38

brooch, which she had worn the day before. She remembered taking it off when she came home from Buckingham Palace. Mr. Openshaw's face contracted into hard lines: grew like what it was before he had known his wife and her child. He rang the bell even before his uncle had done speaking. It was answered by the housemaid.

"Mary, was any one here last night while we were away?"

"A man, sir, came to speak to Norah."

"To speak to Norah! Who was he? How long did he stay?"

"I'm sure I can't tell, sir. He came—perhaps about nine. I went up to tell Norah in the nursery, and she came down to speak to him. She let him out, sir. She will know who he was, and how long he stayed."

She waited a moment to be asked any more questions, but she was not, so she went away.

A minute afterwards Openshaw made as though he were going out of the room; but his wife laid her hand on his arm:

"Do not speak to her before the children," she said, in her low, quiet voice. "I will go up and question her."

"No! I must speak to her. You must know," said he, turning to his uncle and aunt, "my missus has an old servant, as faithful as ever woman was, I do believe, as far as love goes,—but, at the same time, who does not always speak truth, as even the missus must allow. Now, my notion is, that this Norah of ours has been come over by some good-for-nothin chap (for she's at the time o' life when they say women pray for husbands—'any, good Lord, any,') and has let him into our house, and the chap has made off with your brooch, and m'appen many another thing beside. It's only saying that Norah is soft-hearted, and does not stick at a white lie—that's all, missus."

It was curious to notice how his tone, his eyes, his whole face changed as he spoke to his wife; but he was the resolute man through all. She knew better than to oppose him; so she went up-stairs, and told Norah her master wanted to speak to her, and that she would take care of the children in the meanwhile.

Norah rose to go without a word. Her thoughts were these:

"If they tear me to pieces they shall never know through me. He may come,—and then just Lord have mercy upon us all: for some of us are dead folk to a certainty. But he shall do it; not me."

You may fancy, now, her look of determination as she faced her master alone in the dining-room; Mr. and Mrs. Chadwick having left the affair in their nephew's hands, seeing that he took it up with such vehemence.

"Norah! Who was that man that came to my house last night?"

"Man, sir!" As if infinitely; surprised but it was only to gain time.

"Yes; the man whom Mary let in; whom she went up-stairs to the nursery to tell you about; whom you came down to speak to; the same chap, I make no doubt, whom you took into the nursery to have your talk out with; whom Ailsie saw, and afterwards dreamed about; thinking, poor wench! she saw him say his prayers, when nothing, I'll be bound, was farther from his thoughts; who took Mrs. Chadwick's brooch, value ten pounds. Now, Norah! Don't go off! I am as sure as that my name's Thomas Openshaw, that you knew nothing of this robbery. But I do think you've been imposed on, and that's the truth. Some good-for-nothing chap has been making up to you, and you've been just like all other women, and have turned a soft place in your heart to him; and he came last night a-lovyering, and you had him up in the nursery, and he made use

40

of his opportunities, and made off with a few things on his way down! Come, now, Norah: it's no blame to you, only you must not be such a fool again. Tell us," he continued, "what name he gave you, Norah? I'll be bound it was not the right one; but it will be a clue for the police."

Norah drew herself up. "You may ask that question, and taunt me with my being single, and with my credulity, as you will, Master Openshaw. You'll get no answer from me. As for the brooch, and the story of theft and burglary; if any friend ever came to see me (which I defy you to prove, and deny), he'd be just as much above doing such a thing as you yourself, Mr. Openshaw, and more so, too; for I'm not at all sure as everything you have is rightly come by, or would be yours long, if every man had his own." She meant, of course, his wife; but he understood her to refer to his property in goods and chattels.

"Now, my good woman," said he, "I'll just tell you truly, I never trusted you out and out; but my wife liked you, and I thought you had many a good point about you. If you once begin to sauce me, I'll have the police to you, and get out the truth in a court of justice, if you'll not tell it me quietly and civilly here. Now the best thing you can do is quietly to tell me who the fellow is. Look here! a man comes to my house; asks for you; you take him up-stairs, a valuable brooch is missing next day; we know that you, and Mary, and cook, are honest; but you refuse to tell us who the man is. Indeed you've told one lie already about him, saying no one was here last night. Now I just put it to you, what do you think a policeman would say to this, or a magistrate? A magistrate would soon make you tell the truth, my good woman."

"There's never the creature born that should get it out of me," said Norah. "Not unless I choose to tell."

"I've a great mind to see," said Mr. Openshaw, growing angry at

41

the defiance. Then, checking himself, he thought before he spoke again:

"Norah, for your missus's sake I don't want to go to extremities. Be a sensible woman, if you can. It's no great disgrace, after all, to have been taken in. I ask you once more—as a friend—who was this man whom you let into my house last night?"

No answer. He repeated the question in an impatient tone. Still no answer. Norah's lips were set in determination not to speak.

"Then there is but one thing to be done. I shall send for a policeman."

"You will not," said Norah, starting forwards. "You shall not, sir! No policeman shall touch me. I know nothing of the brooch, but I know this: ever since I was four-and-twenty I have thought more of your wife than of myself: ever since I saw her, a poor motherless girl put upon in her uncle's house, I have thought more of serving her than of serving myself! I have cared for her and her child, as nobody ever cared for me. I don't cast blame on you, sir, but I say it's ill giving up one's life to any one; for, at the end, they will turn round upon you, and forsake you. Why does not my missus come herself to suspect me? Maybe she is gone for the police? But I don't stay here, either for police, or magistrate, or master. You're an unlucky lot. I believe there's a curse on you. I'll leave you this very day. Yes! I leave that poor Ailsie, too. I will! No good will ever come to you!"

Mr. Openshaw was utterly astonished at this speech; most of which was completely unintelligible to him, as may easily be supposed. Before he could make up his mind what to say, or what to do, Norah had left the room. I do not think he had ever really intended to send for the police to this old servant of his wife's; for he had never for a moment doubted her perfect honesty. But he had intended to compel her to tell him who the

42

man was, and in this he was baffled. He was, consequently, much irritated. He returned to his uncle and aunt in a state of great annoyance and perplexity, and told them he could get nothing out of the woman; that some man had been in the house the night before; but that she refused to tell who he was. At this moment his wife came in, greatly agitated, and asked what had happened to Norah; for that she had put on her things in passionate haste, and had left the house.

"This looks suspicious," said Mr. Chadwick. "It is not the way in which an honest person would have acted."

Mr. Openshaw kept silence. He was sorely perplexed. But Mrs. Openshaw turned round on Mr. Chadwick with a sudden fierceness no one ever saw in her before.

"You don't know Norah, uncle! She is gone because she is deeply hurt at being suspected. O, I wish I had seen her—that I had spoken to her myself. She would have told me anything." Alice wrung her hands.

"I must confess," continued Mr. Chadwick to his nephew, in a lower voice, "I can't make you out. You used to be a word and a blow, and oftenest the blow first; and now, when there is every cause for suspicion, you just do nought. Your missus is a very good woman, I grant; but she may have been put upon as well as other folk, I suppose. If you don't send for the police, I shall."

"Very well," replied Mr. Openshaw, surlily. "I can't clear Norah. She won't clear herself, as I believe she might if she would. Only I wash my hands of it; for I am sure the woman herself is honest, and she's lived a long time with my wife, and I don't like her to come to shame."

"But she will then be forced to clear herself. That, at any rate, will be a good thing."

"Very well, very well! I am heart-sick of the whole

business. Come, Alice, come up to the babies they'll be in a sore way. I tell you, uncle!" he said, turning round once more to Mr. Chadwick, suddenly and sharply, after his eye had fallen on Alice's wan, tearful, anxious face; "I'll have none sending for the police after all. I'll buy my aunt twice as handsome a brooch this very day; but I'll not have Norah suspected, and my missus plagued. There's for you."

He and his wife left the room. Mr. Chadwick quietly waited till he was out of hearing, and then aid to his wife; "For all Tom's heroics, I'm just quietly going for a detective, wench. Thou need'st know nought about it."

He went to the police-station, and made a statement of the case. He was gratified by the impression which the evidence against Norah seemed to make. The men all agreed in his opinion, and steps were to be immediately taken to find out where she was. Most probably, as they suggested, she had gone at once to the man, who, to all appearance, was her lover. When Mr. Chadwick asked how they would find her out? they smiled, shook their heads, and spoke of mysterious but infallible ways and means. He returned to his nephew's house with a very comfortable opinion of his own sagacity. He was met by his wife with a penitent face:

"O master, I've found my brooch! It was just sticking by its pin in the flounce of my brown silk, that I wore yesterday. I took it off in a hurry, and it must have caught in it; and I hung up my gown in the closet. Just now, when I was going to fold it up, there was the brooch! I'm very vexed, but I never dreamt but what it was lost!"

Her husband muttering something very like "Confound thee and thy brooch too! I wish I'd never given it thee," snatched up his hat, and rushed back to the station; hoping to be in time to stop the police from searching for Norah. But a detective was already gone off on the errand.

Where was Norah? Half mad with the strain of the fearful secret, she had hardly slept through the night for thinking what must be done. Upon this terrible state of mind had come Ailsie's questions, showing that she had seen the Man, as the unconscious child called her father. Lastly came the suspicion of her honesty. She was little less than crazy as she ran up-stairs and dashed on her bonnet and shawl; leaving all else, even her purse, behind her. In that house she would not stay. That was all she knew or was clear about. She would not even see the children again, for fear it should weaken her. She feared above everything Mr. Frank's return to claim his wife. She could not tell what remedy there was for a sorrow so tremendous, for her to stay to witness. The desire of escaping from the coming event was a stronger motive for her departure than her soreness about the suspicions directed against her; although this last had been the final goad to the course she took. She walked away almost at headlong speed; sobbing as she went, as she had not dared to do during the past night for fear of exciting wonder in those who might hear her. Then she stopped. An idea came into her mind that she would leave London altogether, and betake herself to her native town of Liverpool. She felt in her pocket for her purse, as she drew near the Euston Square station with this intention. She had left it at home. Her poor head aching, her eyes swollen with crying, she had to stand still, and think, as well as she could, where next she should bend her steps. Suddenly the thought flashed into her mind that she would go and find out poor Mr. Frank. She had been hardly kind to him the night before, though her heart had bled for him ever since. She remembered his telling her as she inquired for his address, almost as she had pushed him out of the door, of some hotel in a street not far distant from Euston Square. Thither she went: with what intention she hardly knew, but to assuage her conscience by telling him how much she pitied him. In her present state she felt herself unfit to counsel, or restrain, or assist, or do ought else but sympathise and weep. The people of the inn said such a person had been there; had arrived only the day before; had gone out soon after his arrival, leaving his luggage in their care; but had never come back. Norah asked for leave to sit down, and await the gentleman's return. The landlady—pretty secure in the deposit of luggage against any probable injury—showed her into a room, and quietly locked the door on the outside. Norah was utterly worn out, and fell asleep—a shivering, starting, uneasy slumber, which lasted for hours.

The detective, meanwhile, had come up with her some time before she entered the hotel, into which he followed her. Asking the landlady to detain her for an hour or so, without giving any reason beyond showing his authority (which made the landlady applaud herself a good deal for having locked her in), he went back to the police-station to report his proceedings. He could have taken her directly; but his object was, if possible, to trace out the man who was supposed to have committed the robbery. Then he heard of the discovery of the brooch; and consequently did not care to return.

Norah slept till even the summer evening began to close in. Then up. Some one was at the door. It would be Mr. Frank; and she dizzily pushed back her ruffled grey hair, which had fallen over her eyes, and stood looking to see him. Instead, there came in Mr. Openshaw and a policeman.

"This is Norah Kennedy," said Mr. Openshaw.

"O, sir," said Norah, "I did not touch the brooch; indeed I did not. O, sir, I cannot live to be thought so badly of;" and very sick and faint, she suddenly sank down on the ground. To her surprise, Mr. Openshaw raised her up very tenderly. Even the policeman helped to lay her on the sofa; and, at Mr. Openshaw's desire, he went for some wine and sandwiches; for the poor gaunt woman lay there almost as if dead with weariness and exhaustion.

"Norah!" said Mr. Openshaw, in his kindest voice, "the brooch is found. It was hanging to Mrs. Chadwick's gown. I beg your pardon. Most truly I beg your pardon, for having troubled you about it. My wife is almost broken-hearted. Eat, Norah,—or, stay, first drink this glass of wine," said he, lifting her head, pouring a little down her throat.

As she drank, she remembered where she was, and who she was waiting for. She suddenly pushed Mr. Openshaw away, saying, "O, sir, you must go. You must not stop a minute. If he comes back he will kill you."

"Alas, Norah! I do not know who 'he' is. But some one is gone away who will never come back: someone who knew you, and whom I am afraid you cared for."

"I don't understand you, sir," said Norah, her master's kind and sorrowful manner bewildering her yet more than his words. The policeman had left the room at Mr. Openshaw's desire, and they two were alone.

"You know what I mean, when I say some one is gone who will never come back. I mean that he is dead!"

"Who?" said Norah, trembling all over.

"A poor man has been found in the Thames this morning, drowned."

"Did he drown himself?" asked Norah, solemnly.

"God only knows," replied Mr. Openshaw, in the same tone. "Your name and address at our house, were found in his pocket: that, and his purse, were the only things, that were found upon him. I am sorry to say it, my poor Norah; but you are required to go and identify him."

"To what?" asked Norah.

"To say who it is. It is always done, in order that some reason may be discovered for the suicide—if suicide it was. I make no doubt he was the man who came to see you at our house last night. It is very sad, I know." He made pauses between each little clause, in order to try and bring back her senses; which he feared were wandering—so wild and sad was her look.

"Master Openshaw," said she, at last, "I've a dreadful secret to tell you—only you must never breathe it to any one, and you and I must hide it away for ever. I thought to have done it all by myself, but I see I cannot. Yon poor man—yes! the dead, drowned creature is, I fear, Mr. Frank, my mistress's first husband!"

Mr. Openshaw sate down, as if shot. He did not speak; but, after a while, he signed to Norah to go on.

"He came to me the other night—when—God be thanked—you were all away at Richmond. He asked me if his wife was dead or alive. I was a brute, and thought more of our all coming home than of his sore trial: spoke out sharp, and said she was married again, and very content and happy: I all but turned him away: and now he lies dead and cold!"

"God forgive me!" said Mr. Openshaw.

"God forgive us all!" said Norah. "Yon poor man needs forgiveness perhaps less than any one among us. He had been among the savages—shipwrecked—I know not what—and he had written letters which had never reached my poor missus."

"He saw his child!"

"He saw her—yes! I took him up, to give his thoughts another start; for I believed he was going mad on my hands. I came to seek him here, as I more than half promised. My mind misgave me when I heard he had never come in. O, sir I it must be him!"

48

Mr. Openshaw rang the bell. Norah was almost too much stunned to wonder at what he did. He asked for writing materials, wrote a letter, and then said to Norah:

"I am writing to Alice, to say I shall be unavoidably absent for a few days; that I have found you; that you are well, and send her your love, and will come home to-morrow. You must go with me to the Police Court; you must identify the body: I will pay high to keep name; and details out of the papers.

"But where are you going, sir?"

He did not answer her directly. Then he said:

"Norah! I must go with you, and look on the face of the man whom I have so injured,—unwittingly, it is true; but it seems to me as if I had killed him. I will lay his head in the grave, as if he were my only brother: and how he must have hated me! I cannot go home to my wife till all that I can do for him is done. Then I go with a dreadful secret on my mind. I shall never speak of it again, after these days are over. I know you will not, either." He shook hands with her: and they never named the subject again, the one to the other.

Norah went home to Alice the next day. Not a word was said on the cause of her abrupt departure a day or two before. Alice had been charged by her husband in his letter not to allude to the supposed theft of the brooch; so she, implicitly obedient to those whom she loved both by nature and habit, was entirely silent on the subject, only treated Norah with the most tender respect, as if to make up for unjust suspicion.

Nor did Alice inquire into the reason why Mr. Openshaw had been absent during his uncle and aunt's visit, after he had once said that it was unavoidable. He came back, grave and quiet; and, from that time forth, was curiously changed. More thoughtful, and perhaps less active; quite as decided in conduct, but with new and different rules for the guidance of that conduct. Towards Alice he could hardly be more kind than he had always been; but he now seemed to look upon her as some one sacred and to be treated with reverence, as well as tenderness. He throve in business, and made a large fortune, one half of which was settled upon her.

* * *

Long years after these events,—a few months after her mother died, Ailsie and her "father" (as she always called Mr. Openshaw) drove to a cemetery a little way out of town, and she was carried to a certain mound by her maid, who was then sent back to the carriage. There was a head-stone, with F. W. and a date. That was all. Sitting by the grave, Mr. Openshaw told her the story; and for the sad fate of that poor father whom she had never seen, he shed the only tears she ever saw fall from his eyes.

* * *

"A most interesting story, all through," I said, as Jarber folded up the first of his series of discoveries in triumph. "A story that goes straight to the heart—especially at the end. But"—I stopped, and looked at Trottle.

Trottle entered his protest directly in the shape of a cough.

"Well!" I said, beginning to lose my patience. "Don't you see that I want you to speak, and that I don't want you to cough?"

"Quite so, ma'am," said Trottle, in a state of respectful obstinacy which would have upset the temper of a saint. "Relative, I presume, to this story, ma'am?"

"Yes, Yes!" said Jarber. "By all means let us hear what this good man has to say."

"Well, sir," answered Trottle, "I want to know why the House

50

over the way doesn't let, and I don't exactly see how your story answers the question. That's all I have to say, sir."

I should have liked to contradict my opinionated servant, at that moment. But, excellent as the story was in itself, I felt that he had hit on the weak point, so far as Jarber's particular purpose in reading it was concerned.

"And that is what you have to say, is it?" repeated Jarber. "I enter this room announcing that I have a series of discoveries, and you jump instantly to the conclusion that the first of the series exhausts my resources. Have I your permission, dear lady, to enlighten this obtuse person, if possible, by reading Number Two?"

"My work is behindhand, ma'am," said Trottle, moving to the door, the moment I gave Jarber leave to go on.

"Stop where you are," I said, in my most peremptory manner, "and give Mr. Jarber his fair opportunity of answering your objection now you have made it."

Trottle sat down with the look of a martyr, and Jarber began to read with his back turned on the enemy more decidedly than ever.

GOING INTO SOCIETY

At one period of its reverses, the House fell into the occupation of a Showman. He was found registered as its occupier, on the parish books of the time when he rented the House, and there was therefore no need of any clue to his name. But, he himself was less easy to be found; for, he had led a wandering life, and settled people had lost sight of him, and people who plumed themselves on being respectable were shy of admitting that they had ever known anything of him. At last, among the marsh lands near the river's level, that lie about Deptford and the neighbouring market-gardens, a Grizzled Personage in velveteen, with a face so cut up by varieties of weather that he looked as if he had been tattooed, was found smoking a pipe at the door of a wooden house on wheels. The wooden house was laid up in ordinary for the winter, near the mouth of a muddy creek; and everything near it, the foggy river, the misty marshes, and the steaming market-gardens, smoked in company with the grizzled man. In the midst of this smoking party, the funnel-chimney of the wooden house on wheels was not remiss, but took its pipe with the rest in a companionable manner.

On being asked if it were he who had once rented the House to Let, Grizzled Velveteen looked surprised, and said yes. Then his name was Magsman? That was it, Toby Magsman—which lawfully christened Robert; but called in the line, from a infant, Toby. There was nothing agin Toby Magsman, he believed? If there was suspicion of such—mention it!

There was no suspicion of such, he might rest assured. But, some inquiries were making about that House, and would he object to say why he left it?

Not at all; why should he? He left it, along of a Dwarf.

Along of a Dwarf?

Mr. Magsman repeated, deliberately and emphatically, Along of a Dwarf.

Might it be compatible with Mr. Magsman's inclination and convenience to enter, as a favour, into a few particulars?

Mr. Magsman entered into the following particulars.

It was a long time ago, to begin with;—afore lotteries and a deal more was done away with. Mr. Magsman was looking about for a good pitch, and he see that house, and he says to himself, "I'll have you, if you're to be had. If money'll get you, I'll have you."

The neighbours cut up rough, and made complaints; but Mr. Magsman don't know what they *would* have had. It was a lovely thing. First of all, there was the canvass, representin the picter of the Giant, in Spanish trunks and a ruff, who was himself half the heighth of the house, and was run up with a line and pulley to a pole on the roof, so that his Ed was coeval with the parapet. Then, there was the canvass, representin the picter of the Albina lady, showing her white air to the Army and Navy in correct uniform. Then, there was the canvass, representin the picter of the Wild Indian a scalpin a member of some foreign nation. Then, there was the canvass, representin the picter of a child of a British Planter, seized by two Boa Constrictors—not that *we* never had no child, nor no Constrictors neither. Similarly, there was the canvass, representin the picter of the Wild Ass of the Prairies—not that *we* never had no wild asses, nor wouldn't have had 'em at a gift. Last, there was the canvass, representin the picter of the Dwarf, and like him too (considerin), with George the Fourth in such a state of astonishment at him as His Majesty couldn't with his utmost politeness and stoutness express. The front of the House was so covered with canvasses, that there wasn't a spark of daylight ever visible on that side. "MAGSMAN'S AMUSEMENTS," fifteen foot long by two foot high, ran over the front door and parlour winders. The passage was a Arbour of green baize and gardenstuff. A barrel-organ performed there unceasing. And as to respectability,—if threepence ain't respectable, what is?

But, the Dwarf is the principal article at present, and he was worth the money. He was wrote up as MAJOR TPSCHOFFKI, OF THE IMPERIAL BULGRADERIAN BRIGADE. Nobody couldn't pronounce the name, and it never was intended anybody should. The public always turned it, as a regular rule, into Chopski. In the line he was called Chops; partly on that account, and partly because his real name, if he ever had any real name (which was very dubious), was Stakes.

He was a uncommon small man, he really was. Certainly not so small as he was made out to be, but where *is* your Dwarf as is? He was a most uncommon small man, with a most uncommon large Ed; and what he had inside that Ed, nobody ever knowed but himself: even supposin himself to have ever took stock of it, which it would have been a stiff job for even him to do.

The kindest little man as never growed! Spirited, but not proud. When he travelled with the Spotted Baby—though he knowed himself to be a nat'ral Dwarf, and knowed the Baby's spots to be put upon him artificial, he nursed that Baby like a mother. You never heerd him give a ill-name to a Giant. He *did* allow himself to break out into strong language respectin the Fat Lady from Norfolk; but that was an affair of the 'art; and when a man's 'art has been trifled with by a lady, and the preference giv to a Indian, he ain't master of his actions.

He was always in love, of course; every human nat'ral phenomenon is. And he was always in love with a large woman; I never knowed the Dwarf as could be got to love a small one. Which helps to keep 'em the Curiosities they are.

54

One sing'ler idea he had in that Ed of his, which must have meant something, or it wouldn't have been there. It was always his opinion that he was entitled to property. He never would put his name to anything. He had been taught to write, by the young man without arms, who got his living with his toes (quite a writing master *he* was, and taught scores in the line), but Chops would have starved to death, afore he'd have gained a bit of bread by putting his hand to a paper. This is the more curious to bear in mind, because HE had no property, nor hope of property, except his house and a sarser. When I say his house, I mean the box, painted and got up outside like a reg'lar six-roomer, that he used to creep into, with a diamond ring (or quite as good to look at) on his forefinger, and ring a little bell out of what the Public believed to be the Drawing-room winder. And when I say a sarser, I mean a Chaney sarser in which he made a collection for himself at the end of every Entertainment. His cue for that, he took from me: "Ladies and gentlemen, the little man will now walk three times round the Cairawan, and retire behind the curtain." When he said anything important, in private life, he mostly wound it up with this form of words, and they was generally the last thing he said to me at night afore he went to bed.

He had what I consider a fine mind—a poetic mind. His ideas respectin his property never come upon him so strong as when he sat upon a barrel-organ and had the handle turned. Arter the wibration had run through him a little time, he would screech out, "Toby, I feel my property coming—grind away! I'm counting my guineas by thousands, Toby—grind away! Toby, I shall be a man of fortun! I feel the Mint a jingling in me, Toby, and I'm swelling out into the Bank of England!" Such is the influence of music on a poetic mind. Not that he was partial to any other music but a barrel-organ; on the contrary, hated it.

He had a kind of a everlasting grudge agin the Public: which is a thing you may notice in many phenomenons that get their living out of it. What riled him most in the nater of his occupation was, that it kep him out of Society. He was continiwally saying, "Toby, my ambition is, to go into Society. The curse of my position towards the Public is, that it keeps me hout of Society. This don't signify to a low beast of a Indian; he an't formed for Society. This don't signify to a Spotted Baby; *he* an't formed for Society.—I am."

Nobody never could make out what Chops done with his money. He had a good salary, down on the drum every Saturday as the day came round, besides having the run of his teeth—and he was a Woodpecker to eat—but all Dwarfs are. The sarser was a little income, bringing him in so many halfpence that he'd carry 'em for a week together, tied up in a pocket-handkercher. And yet he never had money. And it couldn't be the Fat Lady from Norfolk, as was once supposed; because it stands to reason that when you have a animosity towards a Indian, which makes you grind your teeth at him to his face, and which can hardly hold you from Goosing him audible when he's going through his War-Dance— it stands to reason you wouldn't under them circumstances deprive yourself, to support that Indian in the lap of luxury.

Most unexpected, the mystery come out one day at Egham Races. The Public was shy of bein pulled in, and Chops was ringin his little bell out of his drawing-room winder, and was snarlin to me over his shoulder as he kneeled down with his legs out at the back-door—for he couldn't be shoved into his house without kneeling down, and the premises wouldn't accommodate his legs—was snarlin, "Here's a precious Public for you; why the Devil don't they tumble up?" when a man in the crowd holds up a carrier-pigeon, and cries out, "If there's any person here as has got a ticket, the Lottery's just drawed, and the number as has come up for the great prize is three, seven, forty-two! Three, seven, forty-two!" I was givin the man

56

to the Furies myself, for calling off the Public's attention—for the Public will turn away, at any time, to look at anything in preference to the thing showed 'em; and if you doubt it, get 'em together for any indiwidual purpose on the face of the earth, and send only two people in late, and see if the whole company an't far more interested in takin particular notice of them two than of you—I say, I wasn't best pleased with the man for callin out, and wasn't blessin him in my own mind, when I see Chops's little bell fly out of winder at a old lady, and he gets up and kicks his box over, exposin the whole secret, and he catches hold of the calves of my legs and he says to me, "Carry me into the wan, Toby, and throw a pail of water over me or I'm a dead man, for I've come into my property!"

Twelve thousand odd hundred pound, was Chops's winnins. He had bought a half-ticket for the twenty-five thousand prize, and it had come up. The first use he made of his property, was, to offer to fight the Wild Indian for five hundred pound a side, him with a poisoned darnin-needle and the Indian with a club; but the Indian being in want of backers to that amount, it went no further.

Arter he had been mad for a week—in a state of mind, in short, in which, if I had let him sit on the organ for only two minutes, I believe he would have bust—but we kep the organ from him— Mr. Chops come round, and behaved liberal and beautiful to all. He then sent for a young man he knowed, as had a wery genteel appearance and was a Bonnet at a gaming-booth (most respectable brought up, father havin been imminent in the livery stable line but unfort'nate in a commercial crisis, through paintin a old gray, ginger-bay, and sellin him with a Pedigree), and Mr. Chops said to this Bonnet, who said his name was Normandy, which it wasn't:

"Normandy, I'm a goin into Society. Will you go with me?"

Says Normandy: "Do I understand you, Mr. Chops, to hintimate that the 'ole of the expenses of that move will be borne by yourself?"

"Correct," says Mr. Chops. "And you shall have a Princely allowance too."

The Bonnet lifted Mr. Chops upon a chair, to shake hands with him, and replied in poetry, with his eyes seemingly full of tears:

"My boat is on the shore,
And my bark is on the sea,
And I do not ask for more,
But I'll Go:—along with thee."

They went into Society, in a chay and four grays with silk jackets. They took lodgings in Pall Mall, London, and they blazed away.

In consequence of a note that was brought to Bartlemy Fair in the autumn of next year by a servant, most wonderful got up in milk-white cords and tops, I cleaned myself and went to Pall Mall, one evening appinted. The gentlemen was at their wine arter dinner, and Mr. Chops's eyes was more fixed in that Ed of his than I thought good for him. There was three of 'em (in company, I mean), and I knowed the third well. When last met, he had on a white Roman shirt, and a bishop's mitre covered with leopard-skin, and played the clarionet all wrong, in a band at a Wild Beast Show.

This gent took on not to know me, and Mr. Chops said: "Gentlemen, this is a old friend of former days:" and Normandy looked at me through a eye-glass, and said, "Magsman, glad to see you!"—which I'll take my oath he wasn't. Mr. Chops, to git him convenient to the table, had his chair on a throne (much of the form of George the Fourth's in the canvass), but he hardly appeared to me to be King there in any other pint of view, for his two gentlemen ordered about like Emperors. They was all dressed like May-Day—gorgeous!—And as to Wine, they swam in all sorts.

I made the round of the bottles, first separate (to say I had done it), and then mixed 'em all together (to say I had done it), and then tried two of 'em as half-and-half, and then t'other two. Altogether, I passed a pleasin evenin, but with a tendency to feel muddled, until I considered it good manners to get up and say, "Mr. Chops, the best of friends must part, I thank you for the wariety of foreign drains you have stood so 'ansome, I looks towards you in red wine, and I takes my leave." Mr. Chops replied, "If you'll just hitch me out of this over your right arm, Magsman, and carry me down-stairs, I'll see you out." I said I couldn't think of such a thing, but he would have it, so I lifted him off his throne. He smelt strong of Maideary, and I couldn't help thinking as I carried him down that it was like carrying a large bottle full of wine, with a rayther ugly stopper, a good deal out of proportion.

When I set him on the door-mat in the hall, he kep me close to him by holding on to my coat-collar, and he whispers:

"I ain't 'appy, Magsman."

"What's on your mind, Mr. Chops?"

"They don't use me well. They an't grateful to me. They puts me on the mantel-piece when I won't have in more Champagne-wine, and they locks me in the sideboard when I won't give up my property."

"Get rid of 'em, Mr. Chops."

"I can't. We're in Society together, and what would Society say?"

"Come out of Society!" says I.

"I can't. You don't know what you're talking about. When you have once gone into Society, you mustn't come out of it."

"Then if you'll excuse the freedom, Mr. Chops," were my remark, shaking my head grave, "I think it's a pity you ever went in."

Mr. Chops shook that deep Ed of his, to a surprisin extent, and slapped it half a dozen times with his hand, and with more Wice than I thought were in him. Then, he says, "You're a good fellow, but you don't understand. Good-night, go along. Magsman, the little man will now walk three times round the Cairawan, and retire behind the curtain." The last I see of him on that occasion was his tryin, on the extremest werge of insensibility, to climb up the stairs, one by one, with his hands and knees. They'd have been much too steep for him, if he had been sober; but he wouldn't be helped.

It warn't long after that, that I read in the newspaper of Mr. Chops's being presented at court. It was printed, "It will be recollected"—and I've noticed in my life, that it is sure to be printed that it *will* be recollected, whenever it won't—"that Mr. Chops is the individual of small stature, whose brilliant success in the last State Lottery attracted so much attention." Well, I says to myself, Such is Life! He has been and done it in earnest at last. He has astonished George the Fourth!

(On account of which, I had that canvass new-painted, him with a bag of money in his hand, a presentin it to George the Fourth, and a lady in Ostrich Feathers fallin in love with him in a bag-wig, sword, and buckles correct.)

I took the House as is the subject of present inquiries—though not the honour of bein acquainted—and I run Magsman's Amusements in it thirteen months—sometimes one thing, sometimes another, sometimes nothin particular, but always all the canvasses outside. One night, when we had played the last

60

company out, which was a shy company, through its raining Heavens hard, I was takin a pipe in the one pair back along with the young man with the toes, which I had taken on for a month (though he never drawed—except on paper), and I heard a kickin at the street door. "Halloa!" I says to the young man, "what's up!" He rubs his eyebrows with his toes, and he says, "I can't imagine, Mr. Magsman"—which he never could imagine nothin, and was monotonous company.

The noise not leavin off, I laid down my pipe, and I took up a candle, and I went down and opened the door. I looked out into the street; but nothin could I see, and nothin was I aware of, until I turned round quick, because some creetur run between my legs into the passage. There was Mr. Chops!

"Magsman," he says, "take me, on the old terms, and you've got me; if it's done, say done!"

I was all of a maze, but I said, "Done, sir."

"Done to your done, and double done!" says he. "Have you got a bit of supper in the house?"

Bearin in mind them sparklin warieties of foreign drains as we'd guzzled away at in Pall Mall, I was ashamed to offer him cold sassages and gin-and-water; but he took 'em both and took 'em free; havin a chair for his table, and sittin down at it on a stool, like hold times. I, all of a maze all the while.

It was arter he had made a clean sweep of the sassages (beef, and to the best of my calculations two pound and a quarter), that the wisdom as was in that little man began to come out of him like prespiration.

"Magsman," he says, "look upon me! You see afore you, One as has both gone into Society and come out."

"O! You *are* out of it, Mr. Chops? How did you get out, sir?"

"SOLD OUT!" says he. You never saw the like of the wisdom as his Ed expressed, when he made use of them two words.

"My friend Magsman, I'll impart to you a discovery I've made. It's wallable; it's cost twelve thousand five hundred pound; it may do you good in life—The secret of this matter is, that it ain't so much that a person goes into Society, as that Society goes into a person."

Not exactly keepin up with his meanin, I shook my head, put on a deep look, and said, "You're right there, Mr. Chops."

"Magsman," he says, twitchin me by the leg, "Society has gone into me, to the tune of every penny of my property."

I felt that I went pale, and though nat'rally a bold speaker, I couldn't hardly say, "Where's Normandy?"

"Bolted. With the plate," said Mr. Chops.

"And t'other one?" meaning him as formerly wore the bishop's mitre.

"Bolted. With the jewels," said Mr. Chops.

I sat down and looked at him, and he stood up and looked at me.

"Magsman," he says, and he seemed to myself to get wiser as he got hoarser; "Society, taken in the lump, is all dwarfs. At the court of St. James's, they was all a doing my old business—all a goin three times round the Cairawan, in the hold court-suits and properties. Elsewheres, they was most of 'em ringin their little bells out of make-believes. Everywheres, the sarser was a goin round. Magsman, the sarser is the uniwersal Institution!"

I perceived, you understand, that he was soured by his misfortunes, and I felt for Mr. Chops.

"As to Fat Ladies," he says, giving his head a tremendious one agin the wall, "there's lots of *them* in Society, and worse than the original. *Hers* was a outrage upon Taste — simply a outrage upon Taste — awakenin contempt — carryin its own punishment in the form of a Indian." Here he giv himself another tremendious one. "But *theirs*, Magsman, *theirs* is mercenary outrages. Lay in Cashmeer shawls, buy bracelets, strew 'em and a lot of 'andsome fans and things about your rooms, let it be known that you give away like water to all as come to admire, and the Fat Ladies that don't exhibit for so much down upon the drum, will come from all the pints of the compass to flock about you, whatever you are. They'll drill holes in your 'art, Magsman, like a Cullender. And when you've no more left to give, they'll laugh at you to your face, and leave you to have your bones picked dry by Wulturs, like the dead Wild Ass of the Prairies that you deserve to be!" Here he giv himself the most tremendious one of all, and dropped.

I thought he was gone. His Ed was so heavy, and he knocked it so hard, and he fell so stoney, and the sassagerial disturbance in him must have been so immense, that I thought he was gone. But, he soon come round with care, and he sat up on the floor, and he said to me, with wisdom comin out of his eyes, if ever it come:

"Magsman! The most material difference between the two states of existence through which your unhappy friend has passed;" he reached out his poor little hand, and his tears dropped down on the moustachio which it was a credit to him to have done his best to grow, but it is not in mortals to command success, — "the difference this. When I was out of Society, I was paid light for being seen. When I went into Society, I paid heavy for being seen. I prefer the former, even if I wasn't forced upon it. Give me out through the trumpet, in the hold way, to-morrow."

Arter that, he slid into the line again as easy as if he had been iled all over. But the organ was kep from him, and no allusions was ever made, when a company was in, to his property. He got wiser every day; his views of Society and the Public was luminous, bewilderin, awful; and his Ed got bigger and bigger as his Wisdom expanded it.

He took well, and pulled 'em in most excellent for nine weeks. At the expiration of that period, when his Ed was a sight, he expressed one evenin, the last Company havin been turned out, and the door shut, a wish to have a little music.

"Mr. Chops," I said (I never dropped the "Mr." with him; the world might do it, but not me); "Mr. Chops, are you sure as you are in a state of mind and body to sit upon the organ?"

His answer was this: "Toby, when next met with on the tramp, I forgive her and the Indian. And I am."

It was with fear and trembling that I began to turn the handle; but he sat like a lamb. I will be my belief to my dying day, that I see his Ed expand as he sat; you may therefore judge how great his thoughts was. He sat out all the changes, and then he come off.

"Toby," he says, with a quiet smile, "the little man will now walk three times round the Cairawan, and retire behind the curtain."

When we called him in the morning, we found him gone into a much better Society than mine or Pall Mall's. I giv Mr. Chops as comfortable a funeral as lay in my power, followed myself as Chief, and had the George the Fourth canvass carried first, in the form of a banner. But, the House was so dismal arterwards, that I giv it up, and took to the Wan again.

* * *

"I don't triumph," said Jarber, folding up the second manuscript,

64

and looking hard at Trottle. "I don't triumph over this worthy creature. I merely ask him if he is satisfied now?"

"How can he be anything else?" I said, answering for Trottle, who sat obstinately silent. "This time, Jarber, you have not only read us a delightfully amusing story, but you have also answered the question about the House. Of course it stands empty now. Who would think of taking it after it had been turned into a caravan?" I looked at Trottle, as I said those last words, and Jarber waved his hand indulgently in the same direction.

"Let this excellent person speak," said Jarber. "You were about to say, my good man?" —

"I only wished to ask, sir," said Trottle doggedly, "if you could kindly oblige me with a date or two in connection with that last story?"

"A date!" repeated Jarber. "What does the man want with dates!"

"I should be glad to know, with great respect," persisted Trottle, "if the person named Magsman was the last tenant who lived in the House. It's my opinion—if I may be excused for giving it—that he most decidedly was not."

With those words, Trottle made a low bow, and quietly left the room.

There is no denying that Jarber, when we were left together, looked sadly discomposed. He had evidently forgotten to inquire about dates; and, in spite of his magnificent talk about his series of discoveries, it was quite as plain that the two stories he had just read, had really and truly exhausted his present stock. I thought myself bound, in common gratitude, to help him out of his embarrassment by a timely suggestion. So I proposed that he should come to tea again, on the next Monday evening, the thirteenth, and should make such inquiries in the meantime, as might enable him to dispose triumphantly of Trottle's objection.

He gallantly kissed my hand, made a neat little speech of acknowledgment, and took his leave. For the rest of the week I would not encourage Trottle by allowing him to refer to the House at all. I suspected he was making his own inquiries about dates, but I put no questions to him.

On Monday evening, the thirteenth, that dear unfortunate Jarber came, punctual to the appointed time. He looked so terribly harassed, that he was really quite a spectacle of feebleness and fatigue. I saw, at a glance, that the question of dates had gone against him, that Mr. Magsman had not been the last tenant of the House, and that the reason of its emptiness was still to seek.

"What I have gone through," said Jarber, "words are not eloquent enough to tell. O Sophonisba, I have begun another series of discoveries! Accept the last two as stories laid on your shrine; and wait to blame me for leaving your curiosity unappeased, until you have heard Number Three."

Number Three looked like a very short manuscript, and I said as much. Jarber explained to me that we were to have some poetry this time. In the course of his investigations he had stepped into the Circulating Library, to seek for information on the one important subject. All the Library-people knew about the House was, that a female relative of the last tenant, as they believed, had, just after that tenant left, sent a little manuscript poem to them which she described as referring to events that had actually passed in the House; and which she wanted the proprietor of the Library to publish. She had written no address on her letter; and the proprietor had kept the manuscript ready to be given back to her (the publishing of poems not being in his line) when she might call for it. She had never called for it; and the poem had been lent to Jarber, at his express request, to read to me.

66

Before he began, I rang the bell for Trottle; being determined to have him present at the new reading, as a wholesome check on his obstinacy. To my surprise Peggy answered the bell, and told me, that Trottle had stepped out without saying where. I instantly felt the strongest possible conviction that he was at his old tricks: and that his stepping out in the evening, without leave, meant—Philandering.

Controlling myself on my visitor's account, I dismissed Peggy, stifled my indignation, and prepared, as politely as might be, to listen to Jarber.

THREE EVENINGS IN THE HOUSE

NUMBER ONE

I.

Yes, it look'd dark and dreary
That long and narrow street:
Only the sound of the rain,
And the tramp of passing feet,
The duller glow of the fire,
And gathering mists of night
To mark how slow and weary
The long day's cheerless flight!

II.

Watching the sullen fire,
Hearing the dreary rain,
Drop after drop, run down
On the darkening window-pane;
Chill was the heart of Bertha,
Chill as that winter day,—
For the star of her life had risen
Only to fade away.

III.

The voice that had been so strong
To bid the snare depart,
The true and earnest will,
And the calm and steadfast heart,
Were now weigh'd down by sorrow,
Were quivering now with pain;

68

The clear path now seem'd clouded,
And all her grief in vain.

IV.

Duty, Right, Truth, who promised
To help and save their own,
Seem'd spreading wide their pinions
To leave her there alone.
So, turning from the Present
To well-known days of yore,
She call'd on them to strengthen
And guard her soul once more.

V.

She thought how in her girlhood
Her life was given away,
The solemn promise spoken
She kept so well to-day;
How to her brother Herbert
She had been help and guide,
And how his artist-nature
On her calm strength relied.

VI.

How through life's fret and turmoil
The passion and fire of art
In him was soothed and quicken'd
By her true sister heart;
How future hopes had always
Been for his sake alone;
And now, what strange new feeling
Possess'd her as its own?

VII.

Her home; each flower that breathed there;
The wind's sigh, soft and low;
Each trembling spray of ivy;
The river's murmuring flow;
The shadow of the forest;
Sunset, or twilight dim;
Dear as they were, were dearer
By leaving them for him.

VIII.

And each year as it found her
In the dull, feverish town,
Saw self still more forgotten,
And selfish care kept down
By the calm joy of evening
That brought him to her side,
To warn him with wise counsel,
Or praise with tender pride.

IX.

Her heart, her life, her future,
Her genius, only meant
Another thing to give him,
And be therewith content.
To-day, what words had stirr'd her,
Her soul could not forget?
What dream had fill'd her spirit
With strange and wild regret?

X.

To leave him for another:
Could it indeed be so?
Could it have cost such anguish

To bid this vision go?
Was this her faith? Was Herbert
The second in her heart?
Did it need all this struggle
To bid a dream depart?

XI.

And yet, within her spirit
A far-off land was seen;
A home, which might have held her;
A love, which might have been;
And Life: not the mere being
Of daily ebb and flow,
But Life itself had claim'd her,
And she had let it go!

XII.

Within her heart there echo'd
Again the well-known tune
That promised this bright future,
And ask'd her for its own:
Then words of sorrow, broken
By half-reproachful pain;
And then a farewell, spoken
In words of cold disdain.

XIII.

Where now was the stern purpose
That nerved her soul so long?
Whence came the words she utter'd,
So hard, so cold, so strong?
What right had she to banish
A hope that God had given?
Why must she choose earth's portion,
And turn aside from Heaven?

XIV.

To-day! Was it this morning?
If this long, fearful strife
Was but the work of hours,
What would be years of life?
Why did a cruel Heaven
For such great suffering call?
And why—O, still more cruel!—
Must her own words do all?

XV.

Did she repent? O Sorrow!
Why do we linger still
To take thy loving message,
And do thy gentle will?
See, her tears fall more slowly;
The passionate murmurs cease,
And back upon her spirit
Flow strength, and love, and peace.

XVI.

The fire burns more brightly,
The rain has passed away,
Herbert will see no shadow
Upon his home to-day;
Only that Bertha greets him
With doubly tender care,
Kissing a fonder blessing
Down on his golden hair.

72

NUMBER TWO.

I.

The studio is deserted,
Palette and brush laid by,
The sketch rests on the easel,
The paint is scarcely dry;
And Silence—who seems always
Within her depths to bear
The next sound that will utter—
Now holds a dumb despair.

II.

So Bertha feels it: listening
With breathless, stony fear,
Waiting the dreadful summons
Each minute brings more near:
When the young life, now ebbing,
Shall fail, and pass away
Into that mighty shadow
Who shrouds the house to-day.

III.

But why—when the sick chamber
Is on the upper floor—
Why dares not Bertha enter
Within the close-shut door?
If he—her all—her Brother,
Lies dying in that gloom,
What strange mysterious power
Has sent her from the room?

IV.

It is not one week's anguish

That can have changed her so;
Joy has not died here lately,
Struck down by one quick blow;
But cruel months have needed
Their long relentless chain,
To teach that shrinking manner
Of helpless, hopeless pain.

V.

The struggle was scarce over
Last Christmas Eve had brought:
The fibres still were quivering
Of the one wounded thought,
When Herbert—who, unconscious,
Had guessed no inward strife—
Bade her, in pride and pleasure,
Welcome his fair young wife.

VI.

Bade her rejoice, and smiling,
Although his eyes were dim,
Thank'd God he thus could pay her
The care she gave to him.
This fresh bright life would bring her
A new and joyous fate—
O Bertha, check the murmur
That cries, Too late! too late!

VII.

Too late! Could she have known it
A few short weeks before,
That his life was completed,
And needing hers no more,
She might—O sad repining!

What "might have been," forget;
"It was not," should suffice us
To stifle vain regret.

VIII.

He needed her no longer,
Each day it grew more plain;
First with a startled wonder,
Then with a wondering pain.
Love: why, his wife best gave it;
Comfort: durst Bertha speak?
Counsel: when quick resentment
Flush'd on the young wife's cheek.

IX.

No more long talks by firelight
Of childish times long past,
And dreams of future greatness
Which he must reach at last;
Dreams, where her purer instinct
With truth unerring told
Where was the worthless gilding,
And where refinèd gold.

X.

Slowly, but surely ever,
Dora's poor jealous pride,
Which she call'd love for Herbert,
Drove Bertha from his side;
And, spite of nervous effort
To share their alter'd life,
She felt a check to Herbert,
A burden to his wife.

XI.

This was the least; for Bertha
Fear'd, dreaded, *knew* at length,
How much his nature owed her
Of truth, and power, and strength;
And watch'd the daily failing
Of all his nobler part:
Low aims, weak purpose, telling
In lower, weaker art.

XII.

And now, when he is dying,
The last words she could hear
Must not be hers, but given
The bride of one short year.
The last care is another's;
The last prayer must not be
The one they learnt together
Beside their mother's knee.

XIII.

Summon'd at last: she kisses
The clay-cold stiffening hand;
And, reading pleading efforts
To make her understand,
Answers, with solemn promise,
In clear but trembling tone,
To Dora's life henceforward
She will devote her own.

XIV.

Now all is over. Bertha
Dares not remain to weep,
But soothes the frightened Dora

Into a sobbing sleep.
The poor weak child will need her:
O, who can dare complain,
When God sends a new Duty
To comfort each new Pain!

NUMBER THREE

I.

The House is all deserted
In the dim evening gloom,
Only one figure passes
Slowly from room to room;
And, pausing at each doorway,
Seems gathering up again
Within her heart the relics
Of bygone joy and pain.

II.

There is an earnest longing
In those who onward gaze,
Looking with weary patience
Towards the coming days.
There is a deeper longing,
More sad, more strong, more keen:
Those know it who look backward,
And yearn for what has been.

III.

At every hearth she pauses,
Touches each well-known chair;
Gazes from every window,
Lingers on every stair.

What have these months brought Bertha
Now one more year is past?
This Christmas Eve shall tell us,
The third one and the last.

IV.

The wilful, wayward Dora,
In those first weeks of grief,
Could seek and find in Bertha
Strength, soothing, and relief.
And Bertha—last sad comfort
True woman-heart can take—
Had something still to suffer
And do for Herbert's sake.

V.

Spring, with her western breezes,
From Indian islands bore
To Bertha news that Leonard
Would seek his home once more.
What was it—joy, or sorrow?
What were they—hopes, or fears?
That flush'd her cheeks with crimson,
And fill'd her eyes with tears?

VI.

He came. And who so kindly
Could ask and hear her tell
Herbert's last hours; for Leonard
Had known and loved him well.
Daily he came; and Bertha,
Poor wear heart, at length,
Weigh'd down by other's weakness,
Could rest upon his strength.

VII.

Yet not the voice of Leonard
Could her true care beguile,
That turn'd to watch, rejoicing,
Dora's reviving smile.
So, from that little household
The worst gloom pass'd away,
The one bright hour of evening
Lit up the livelong day.

VIII.

Days passed. The golden summer
In sudden heat bore down
Its blue, bright, glowing sweetness
Upon the scorching town.
And sights and sounds of country
Came in the warm soft tune
Sung by the honey'd breezes
Borne on the wings of June.

IX.

One twilight hour, but earlier
Than usual, Bertha thought
She knew the fresh sweet fragrance
Of flowers that Leonard brought;
Through open'd doors and windows
It stole up through the gloom,
And with appealing sweetness
Drew Bertha from her room.

X.

Yes, he was there; and pausing
Just near the open'd door,
To check her heart's quick beating,

She heard—and paused still more—
His low voice Dora's answers—
His pleading—Yes, she knew
The tone—the words—the accents:
She once had heard them too.

XI.

"Would Bertha blame her?" Leonard's
Low, tender answer came:
"Bertha was far too noble
To think or dream of blame."
"And was he sure he loved her?"
"Yes, with the one love given
Once in a lifetime only,
With one soul and one heaven!"

XII.

Then came a plaintive murmur,—
"Dora had once been told
That he and Bertha—" "Dearest,
Bertha is far too cold
To love; and I, my Dora,
If once I fancied so,
It was a brief delusion,
And over,—long ago."

XIII.

Between the Past and Present,
On that bleak moment's height,
She stood. As some lost traveller
By a quick flash of light
Seeing a gulf before him,
With dizzy, sick despair,
Reels to clutch backward, but to find
A deeper chasm there.

XIV.

The twilight grew still darker,
The fragrant flowers more sweet,
The stars shone out in heaven,
The lamps gleam'd down the street;
And hours pass'd in dreaming
Over their new-found fate,
Ere they could think of wondering
Why Bertha was so late.

XV.

She came, and calmly listen'd;
In vain they strove to trace
If Herbert's memory shadow'd
In grief upon her face.
No blame, no wonder show'd there,
No feeling could be told;
Her voice was not less steady,
Her manner not more cold.

XVI.

They could not hear the anguish
That broke in words of pain
Through that calm summer midnight, —
"My Herbert — mine again!"
Yes, they have once been parted,
But this day shall restore
The long lost one: she claims him:
"My Herbert — mine once more!"

XVII.

Now Christmas Eve returning,
Saw Bertha stand beside
The altar, greeting Dora,

Again a smiling bride;
And now the gloomy evening
Sees Bertha pale and worn,
Leaving the house for ever,
To wander out forlorn.

XVIII.

Forlorn—nay, not so. Anguish
Shall do its work at length;
Her soul, pass'd through the fire,
Shall gain still purer strength.
Somewhere there waits for Bertha
An earnest noble part;
And, meanwhile, God is with her,—
God, and her own true heart!

** * *

I could warmly and sincerely praise the little poem, when Jarber had done reading it; but I could not say that it tended in any degree towards clearing up the mystery of the empty House.

Whether it was the absence of the irritating influence of Trottle, or whether it was simply fatigue, I cannot say, but Jarber did not strike me, that evening, as being in his usual spirits. And though he declared that he was not in the least daunted by his want of success thus far, and that he was resolutely determined to make more discoveries, he spoke in a languid absent manner, and shortly afterwards took his leave at rather an early hour.

When Trottle came back, and when I indignantly taxed him with Philandering, he not only denied the imputation, but asserted that he had been employed on my service, and, in consideration of that, boldly asked for leave of absence for two days, and for a morning to himself afterwards, to complete the business, in which he solemnly declared that I was interested. In remembrance of his long and faithful service to me, I did violence to myself, and granted his request. And he, on his side, engaged to explain himself to my satisfaction, in a week's time, on Monday evening the twentieth.

A day or two before, I sent to Jarber's lodgings to ask him to drop in to tea. His landlady sent back an apology for him that made my hair stand on end. His feet were in hot water; his head was in a flannel petticoat; a green shade was over his eyes; the rheumatism was in his legs; and a mustard-poultice was on his chest. He was also a little feverish, and rather distracted in his mind about Manchester Marriages, a Dwarf, and Three Evenings, or Evening Parties—his landlady was not sure which—in an empty House, with the Water Rate unpaid.

Under these distressing circumstances, I was necessarily left alone with Trottle. His promised explanation began, like Jarber's discoveries, with the reading of a written paper. The only difference was that Trottle introduced his manuscript under the name of a Report.

TROTTLE'S REPORT

The curious events related in these pages would, many of them, most likely never have happened, if a person named Trottle had not presumed, contrary to his usual custom, to think for himself.

The subject on which the person in question had ventured, for the first time in his life, to form an opinion purely and entirely his own, was one which had already excited the interest of his respected mistress in a very extraordinary degree. Or, to put it in plainer terms still, the subject was no other than the mystery of the empty House.

Feeling no sort of objection to set a success of his own, if possible, side by side with a failure of Mr. Jarber's, Trottle made up his mind, one Monday evening, to try what he could do, on his own account, towards clearing up the mystery of the empty House. Carefully dismissing from his mind all nonsensical notions of former tenants and their histories, and keeping the one point in view steadily before him, he started to reach it in the shortest way, by walking straight up to the House, and bringing himself face to face with the first person in it who opened the door to him.

It was getting towards dark, on Monday evening, the thirteenth of the month, when Trottle first set foot on the steps of the House. When he knocked at the door, he knew nothing of the matter which he was about to investigate, except that the landlord was an elderly widower of good fortune, and that his name was Forley. A small beginning enough for a man to start from, certainly!

On dropping the knocker, his first proceeding was to look down cautiously out of the corner of his right eye, for any results which might show themselves at the kitchen-window. There appeared at it immediately the figure of a woman, who looked up inquisitively at the stranger on the steps, left the window in a hurry, and came back to it with an open letter in her hand, which she held up to the fading light. After looking over the letter hastily for a moment or so, the woman disappeared once more.

Trottle next heard footsteps shuffling and scraping along the bare hall of the house. On a sudden they ceased, and the sound of two voices—a shrill persuading voice and a gruff resisting voice—confusedly reached his ears. After a while, the voices left off speaking—a chain was undone, a bolt drawn back—the door opened—and Trottle stood face to face with two persons, a woman in advance, and a man behind her, leaning back flat against the wall.

"Wish you good evening, sir," says the woman, in such a sudden way, and in such a cracked voice, that it was quite startling to hear her. "Chilly weather, ain't it, sir? Please to walk in. You come from good Mr. Forley, don't you, sir?"

"Don't you, sir?" chimes in the man hoarsely, making a sort of gruff echo of himself, and chuckling after it, as if he thought he had made a joke.

If Trottle had said, "No," the door would have been probably closed in his face. Therefore, he took circumstances as he found them, and boldly ran all the risk, whatever it might be, of saying, "Yes."

"Quite right sir," says the woman. "Good Mr. Forley's letter told us his particular friend would be here to represent him, at dusk, on Monday the thirteenth—or, if not on Monday the thirteenth, then on Monday the twentieth, at the same time, without fail. And here you are on Monday the thirteenth, ain't you, sir? Mr. Forley's particular friend, and dressed all in black— quite right, sir! Please to step into the dining-room—it's always

85

kept scoured and clean against Mr. Forley comes here—and I'll fetch a candle in half a minute. It gets so dark in the evenings, now, you hardly know where you are, do you, sir? And how is good Mr. Forley in his health? We trust he is better, Benjamin, don't we? We are so sorry not to see him as usual, Benjamin, ain't we? In half a minute, sir, if you don't mind waiting, I'll be back with the candle. Come along, Benjamin."

"Come along, Benjamin," chimes in the echo, and chuckles again as if he thought he had made another joke.

Left alone in the empty front-parlour, Trottle wondered what was coming next, as he heard the shuffling, scraping footsteps go slowly down the kitchen-stairs. The front-door had been carefully chained up and bolted behind him on his entrance; and there was not the least chance of his being able to open it to effect his escape, without betraying himself by making a noise.

Not being of the Jarber sort, luckily for himself, he took his situation quietly, as he found it, and turned his time, while alone, to account, by summing up in his own mind the few particulars which he had discovered thus far. He had found out, first, that Mr. Forley was in the habit of visiting the house regularly. Second, that Mr. Forley being prevented by illness from seeing the people put in charge as usual, had appointed a friend to represent him; and had written to say so. Third, that the friend had a choice of two Mondays, at a particular time in the evening, for doing his errand; and that Trottle had accidentally hit on this time, and on the first of the Mondays, for beginning his own investigations. Fourth, that the similarity between Trottle's black dress, as servant out of livery, and the dress of the messenger (whoever he might be), had helped the error by which Trottle was profiting. So far, so good. But what was the messenger's errand? and what chance was there that he might not come up and knock at the door himself, from minute to minute, on that very evening?

86

While Trottle was turning over this last consideration in his mind, he heard the shuffling footsteps come up the stairs again, with a flash of candle-light going before them. He waited for the woman's coming in with some little anxiety; for the twilight had been too dim on his getting into the house to allow him to see either her face or the man's face at all clearly.

The woman came in first, with the man she called Benjamin at her heels, and set the candle on the mantel-piece. Trottle takes leave to describe her as an offensively-cheerful old woman, awfully lean and wiry, and sharp all over, at eyes, nose, and chin—devilishly brisk, smiling, and restless, with a dirty false front and a dirty black cap, and short fidgetty arms, and long hooked finger-nails—an unnaturally lusty old woman, who walked with a spring in her wicked old feet, and spoke with a smirk on her wicked old face—the sort of old woman (as Trottle thinks) who ought to have lived in the dark ages, and been ducked in a horse-pond, instead of flourishing in the nineteenth century, and taking charge of a Christian house.

"You'll please to excuse my son, Benjamin, won't you, sir?" says this witch without a broomstick, pointing to the man behind her, propped against the bare wall of the dining-room, exactly as he had been propped against the bare wall of the passage. "He's got his inside dreadful bad again, has my son Benjamin. And he won't go to bed, and he will follow me about the house, up-stairs and downstairs, and in my lady's chamber, as the song says, you know. It's his indisgestion, poor dear, that sours his temper and makes him so agravating—and indisgestion is a wearing thing to the best of us, ain't it, sir?"

"Ain't it, sir?" chimes in agravating Benjamin, winking at the candle-light like an owl at the sunshine.

Trottle examined the man curiously, while his horrid old mother was speaking of him. He found "My son Benjamin" to be little and lean, and buttoned-up slovenly in a frowsy old great-coat that fell down to his ragged carpet-slippers. His eyes were very watery, his cheeks very pale, and his lips very red. His breathing was so uncommonly loud, that it sounded almost like a snore. His head rolled helplessly in the monstrous big collar of his great-coat; and his limp, lazy hands pottered about the wall on either side of him, as if they were groping for a imaginary bottle. In plain English, the complaint of "My son Benjamin" was drunkenness, of the stupid, pig-headed, sottish kind. Drawing this conclusion easily enough, after a moment's observation of the man, Trottle found himself, nevertheless, keeping his eyes fixed much longer than was necessary on the ugly drunken face rolling about in the monstrous big coat collar, and looking at it with a curiosity that he could hardly account for at first. Was there something familiar to him in the man's features? He turned away from them for an instant, and then turned back to him again. After that second look, the notion forced itself into his mind, that he had certainly seen a face somewhere, of which that sot's face appeared like a kind of slovenly copy. "Where?" thinks he to himself, "where did I last see the man whom this agravating Benjamin, here, so very strongly reminds me of?"

It was no time, just then—with the cheerful old woman's eye searching him all over, and the cheerful old woman's tongue talking at him, nineteen to the dozen—for Trottle to be ransacking his memory for small matters that had got into wrong corners of it. He put by in his mind that very curious circumstance respecting Benjamin's face, to be taken up again when a fit opportunity offered itself; and kept his wits about him in prime order for present necessities.

"You wouldn't like to go down into the kitchen, would you?" says the witch without the broomstick, as familiar as if she had been Trottle's mother, instead of Benjamin's. "There's a bit of fire in the grate, and the sink in the back kitchen don't smell to matter much to-day, and it's uncommon chilly up here when a

88

person's flesh don't hardly cover a person's bones. But you don't look cold, sir, do you? And then, why, Lord bless my soul, our little bit of business is so very, very little, it's hardly worth while to go downstairs about it, after all. Quite a game at business, ain't it, sir? Give-and-take that's what I call it—give-and-take!"

With that, her wicked old eyes settled hungrily on the region round about Trottle's waistcoat-pocket, and she began to chuckle like her son, holding out one of her skinny hands, and tapping cheerfully in the palm with the knuckles of the other. Agravating Benjamin, seeing what she was about, roused up a little, chuckled and tapped in imitation of her, got an idea of his own into his muddled head all of a sudden, and bolted it out charitably for the benefit of Trottle.

"I say!" says Benjamin, settling himself against the wall and nodding his head viciously at his cheerful old mother. "I say! Look out. She'll skin you!"

Assisted by these signs and warnings, Trottle found no difficulty in understanding that the business referred to was the giving and taking of money, and that he was expected to be the giver. It was at this stage of the proceedings that he first felt decidedly uncomfortable, and more than half inclined to wish he was on the street-side of the house-door again.

He was still cudgelling his brains for an excuse to save his pocket, when the silence was suddenly interrupted by a sound in the upper part of the house.

It was not at all loud—it was a quiet, still, scraping sound—so faint that it could hardly have reached the quickest ears, except in an empty house.

"Do you hear that, Benjamin?" says the old woman. "He's at it again, even in the dark, ain't he? P'raps you'd like to see him, sir!" says she, turning on Trottle, and poking her grinning face close to him. "Only name it; only say if you'd like to see him before we do our little bit of business—and I'll show good Forley's friend up-stairs, just as if he was good Mr. Forley himself. *My* legs are all right, whatever Benjamin's may be. I get younger and younger, and stronger and stronger, and jollier and jollier, every day—that's what I do! Don't mind the stairs on my account, sir, if you'd like to see him."

"Him?" Trottle wondered whether "him" meant a man, or a boy, or a domestic animal of the male species. Whatever it meant, here was a chance of putting off that uncomfortable give-and-take-business, and, better still, a chance perhaps of finding out one of the secrets of the mysterious House. Trottle's spirits began to rise again and he said "Yes," directly, with the confidence of a man who knew all about it.

Benjamin's mother took the candle at once, and lighted Trottle briskly to the stairs; and Benjamin himself tried to follow as usual. But getting up several flights of stairs, even helped by the bannisters, was more, with his particular complaint, than he seemed to feel himself inclined to venture on. He sat down obstinately on the lowest step, with his head against the wall, and the tails of his big great-coat spreading out magnificently on the stairs behind him and above him, like a dirty imitation of a court lady's train.

"Don't sit there, dear," says his affectionate mother, stopping to snuff the candle on the first landing.

"I shall sit here," says Benjamin, agravating to the last, "till the milk comes in the morning."

The cheerful old woman went on nimbly up the stairs to the first floor, and Trottle followed, with his eyes and ears wide open. He had seen nothing out of the common in the front-parlour, or up the staircase, so far. The House was dirty and

90

dreary and close-smelling—but there was nothing about it to excite the least curiosity, except the faint scraping sound, which was now beginning to get a little clearer—though still not at all loud—as Trottle followed his leader up the stairs to the second floor.

Nothing on the second-floor landing, but cobwebs above and bits of broken plaster below, cracked off from the ceiling. Benjamin's mother was not a bit out of breath, and looked all ready to go to the top of the monument if necessary. The faint scraping sound had got a little clearer still; but Trottle was no nearer to guessing what it might be, than when he first heard it in the parlour downstairs.

On the third, and last, floor, there were two doors; one, which was shut, leading into the front garret; and one, which was ajar, leading into the back garret. There was a loft in the ceiling above the landing; but the cobwebs all over it vouched sufficiently for its not having been opened for some little time. The scraping noise, plainer than ever here, sounded on the other side of the back garret door; and, to Trottle's great relief, that was precisely the door which the cheerful old woman now pushed open.

Trottle followed her in; and, for once in his life, at any rate, was struck dumb with amazement, at the sight which the inside of the room revealed to him.

The garret was absolutely empty of everything in the shape of furniture. It must have been used at one time or other, by somebody engaged in a profession or a trade which required for the practice of it a great deal of light; for the one window in the room, which looked out on a wide open space at the back of the house, was three or four times as large, every way, as a garret-window usually is. Close under this window, kneeling on the bare boards with his face to the door, there appeared, of all the creatures in the world to see alone at such a place and at such a time, a mere mite of a child—a little, lonely, wizen, strangely-

91

clad boy, who could not at the most, have been more than five years old. He had a greasy old blue shawl crossed over his breast, and rolled up, to keep the ends from the ground, into a great big lump on his back. A strip of something which looked like the remains of a woman's flannel petticoat, showed itself under the shawl, and, below that again, a pair of rusty black stockings, worlds too large for him, covered his legs and his shoeless feet. A pair of old clumsy muffetees, which had worked themselves up on his little frail red arms to the elbows, and a big cotton nightcap that had dropped down to his very eyebrows, finished off the strange dress which the poor little man seemed not half big enough to fill out, and not near strong enough to walk about in.

But there was something to see even more extraordinary than the clothes the child was swaddled up in, and that was the game which he was playing at, all by himself; and which, moreover, explained in the most unexpected manner the faint scraping noise that had found its way down-stairs, through the half-opened door, in the silence of the empty house.

It has been mentioned that the child was on his knees in the garret, when Trottle first saw him. He was not saying his prayers, and not crouching down in terror at being alone in the dark. He was, odd and unaccountable as it may appear, doing nothing more or less than playing at a charwoman's or housemaid's business of scouring the floor. Both his little hands had tight hold of a mangy old blacking-brush, with hardly any bristles left in it, which he was rubbing backwards and forwards on the boards, as gravely and steadily as if he had been at scouring-work for years, and had got a large family to keep by it. The coming-in of Trottle and the old woman did not startle or disturb him in the least. He just looked up for a minute at the candle, with a pair of very bright, sharp eyes, and then went on with his work again, as if nothing had happened. On one side of him was a battered pint saucepan without a handle, which was

92

his make-believe pail; and on the other a morsel of slate-coloured cotton rag, which stood for his flannel to wipe up with. After scrubbing bravely for a minute or two, he took the bit of rag, and mopped up, and then squeezed make-believe water out into his make-believe pail, as grave as any judge that ever sat on a Bench. By the time he thought he had got the floor pretty dry, he raised himself upright on his knees, and blew out a good long breath, and set his little red arms akimbo, and nodded at Trottle.

"There!" says the child, knitting his little downy eyebrows into a frown. "Drat the dirt! I've cleaned up. Where's my beer?"

Benjamin's mother chuckled till Trottle thought she would have choked herself.

"Lord ha' mercy on us!" says she, "just hear the imp. You would never think he was only five years old, would you, sir? Please to tell good Mr. Forley you saw him going on as nicely as ever, playing at being me scouring the parlour floor, and calling for my beer afterwards. That's his regular game, morning, noon, and night—he's never tired of it. Only look how snug we've been and dressed him. That's my shawl a keepin his precious little body warm, and Benjamin's nightcap a keepin his precious little head warm, and Benjamin's stockings, drawed over his trowsers, a keepin his precious little legs warm. He's snug and happy if ever a imp was yet. 'Where's my beer!'—say it again, little dear, say it again!"

If Trottle had seen the boy, with a light and a fire in the room, clothed like other children, and playing naturally with a top, or a box of soldiers, or a bouncing big India-rubber ball, he might have been as cheerful under the circumstances as Benjamin's mother herself. But seeing the child reduced (as he could not help suspecting) for want of proper toys and proper child's company, to take up with the mocking of an old woman at her scouring-work, for something to stand in the place of a game,

Trottle, though not a family man, nevertheless felt the sight before him to be, in its way, one of the saddest and the most pitiable that he had ever witnessed.

"Why, my man," says he, "you're the boldest little chap in all England. You don't seem a bit afraid of being up here all by yourself in the dark."

"The big winder," says the child, pointing up to it, "sees in the dark; and I see with the big winder." He stops a bit, and gets up on his legs, and looks hard at Benjamin's mother. "I'm a good 'un," says he, "ain't I? I save candle."

Trottle wondered what else the forlorn little creature had been brought up to do without, besides candle-light; and risked putting a question as to whether he ever got a run in the open air to cheer him up a bit. O, yes, he had a run now and then, out of doors (to say nothing of his runs about the house), the lively little cricket—a run according to good Mr. Forley's instructions, which were followed out carefully, as good Mr. Forley's friend would be glad to hear, to the very letter.

As Trottle could only have made one reply to this, namely, that good Mr. Forley's instructions were, in his opinion, the instructions of an infernal scamp; and as he felt that such an answer would naturally prove the death-blow to all further discoveries on his part, he gulped down his feelings before they got too many for him, and held his tongue, and looked round towards the window again to see what the forlorn little boy was going to amuse himself with next.

The child had gathered up his blacking-brush and bit of rag, and had put them into the old tin saucepan; and was now working his way, as well as his clothes would let him, with his make-believe pail hugged up in his arms, towards a door of communication which led from the back to the front garret.

"I say," says he, looking round sharply over his shoulder, "what are you two stopping here for? I'm going to bed now—and so I tell you!"

With that, he opened the door, and walked into the front room. Seeing Trottle take a step or two to follow him, Benjamin's mother opened her wicked old eyes in a state of great astonishment.

"Mercy on us!" says she, "haven't you seen enough of him yet?"

"No," says Trottle. "I should like to see him go to bed."

Benjamin's mother burst into such a fit of chuckling that the loose extinguisher in the candlestick clattered again with the shaking of her hand. To think of good Mr. Forley's friend taking ten times more trouble about the imp than good Mr. Forley himself! Such a joke as that, Benjamin's mother had not often met with in the course of her life, and she begged to be excused if she took the liberty of having a laugh at it.

Leaving her to laugh as much as she pleased, and coming to a pretty positive conclusion, after what he had just heard, that Mr. Forley's interest in the child was not of the fondest possible kind, Trottle walked into the front room, and Benjamin's mother, enjoying herself immensely, followed with the candle.

There were two pieces of furniture in the front garret. One, an old stool of the sort that is used to stand a cask of beer on; and the other a great big ricketty straddling old truckle bedstead. In the middle of this bedstead, surrounded by a dim brown waste of sacking, was a kind of little island of poor bedding—an old bolster, with nearly all the feathers out of it, doubled in three for a pillow; a mere shred of patchwork counter-pane, and a blanket; and under that, and peeping out a little on either side beyond the loose clothes, two faded chair cushions of horsehair, laid along together for a sort of makeshift mattress. When

Trottle got into the room, the lonely little boy had scrambled up on the bedstead with the help of the beer-stool, and was kneeling on the outer rim of sacking with the shred of counterpane in his hands, just making ready to tuck it in for himself under the chair cushions.

"I'll tuck you up, my man," says Trottle. "Jump into bed, and let me try."

"I mean to tuck myself up," says the poor forlorn child, "and I don't mean to jump. I mean to crawl, I do—and so I tell you!"

With that, he set to work, tucking in the clothes tight all down the sides of the cushions, but leaving them open at the foot. Then, getting up on his knees, and looking hard at Trottle as much as to say, "What do you mean by offering to help such a handy little chap as me?" he began to untie the big shawl for himself, and did it, too, in less than half a minute. Then, doubling the shawl up loose over the foot of the bed, he says, "I say, look here," and ducks under the clothes, head first, worming his way up and up softly, under the blanket and counterpane, till Trottle saw the top of the large nightcap slowly peep out on the bolster. This over-sized head-gear of the child's had so shoved itself down in the course of his journey to the pillow, under the clothes, that when he got his face fairly out on the bolster, he was all nightcap down to his mouth. He soon freed himself, however, from this slight encumbrance by turning the ends of the cap up gravely to their old place over his eyebrows—looked at Trottle—said, "Snug, ain't it? Good-bye!"—popped his face under the clothes again—and left nothing to be seen of him but the empty peak of the big nightcap standing up sturdily on end in the middle of the bolster.

"What a young limb it is, ain't it?" says Benjamin's mother, giving Trottle a cheerful dig with her elbow. "Come on! you won't see no more of him to-night!"

"And so I tell you!" sings out a shrill, little voice under the bedclothes, chiming in with a playful finish to the old woman's last words.

If Trottle had not been, by this time, positively resolved to follow the wicked secret which accident had mixed him up with, through all its turnings and windings, right on to the end, he would have probably snatched the boy up then and there, and carried him off from his garret prison, bed-clothes and all. As it was, he put a strong check on himself, kept his eye on future possibilities, and allowed Benjamin's mother to lead him downstairs again.

"Mind them top bannisters," says she, as Trottle laid his hand on them. "They are as rotten as medlars every one of 'em."

"When people come to see the premises," says Trottle, trying to feel his way a little farther into the mystery of the House, "you don't bring many of them up here, do you?"

"Bless your heart alive!" says she, "nobody ever comes now. The outside of the house is quite enough to warn them off. Mores the pity, as I say. It used to keep me in spirits, staggering 'em all, one after another, with the frightful high rent—specially the women, drat 'em. 'What's the rent of this house?'—'Hundred and twenty pound a-year!'—'Hundred and twenty? why, there ain't a house in the street as lets for more than eighty!'—Likely enough, ma'am; other landlords may lower their rents if they please; but this here landlord sticks to his rights, and means to have as much for his house as his father had before him!'—'But the neighbourhood's gone off since then!'—'Hundred and twenty pound, ma'am.'—'The landlord must be mad!'—'Hundred and twenty pound, ma'am.'—'Open the door you impertinent woman!' Lord! what a happiness it was to see 'em bounce out, with that awful rent a-ringing in their ears all down the street!"

97

She stopped on the second-floor landing to treat herself to another chuckle, while Trottle privately posted up in his memory what he had just heard. "Two points made out," he thought to himself: "the house is kept empty on purpose, and the way it's done is to ask a rent that nobody will pay."

"Ah, deary me!" says Benjamin's mother, changing the subject on a sudden, and twisting back with a horrid, greedy quickness to those awkward money-matters which she had broached down in the parlour. "What we've done, one way and another for Mr. Forley, it isn't in words to tell! That nice little bit of business of ours ought to be a bigger bit of business, considering the trouble we take, Benjamin and me, to make the imp upstairs as happy as the day is long. If good Mr. Forley would only please to think a little more of what a deal he owes to Benjamin and me—"

"That's just it," says Trottle, catching her up short in desperation, and seeing his way, by the help of those last words of hers, to slipping cleverly through her fingers. "What should you say, if I told you that Mr. Forley was nothing like so far from thinking about that little matter as you fancy? You would be disappointed, now, if I told you that I had come to-day without the money?"—(her lank old jaw fell, and her villainous old eyes glared, in a perfect state of panic, at that!)—"But what should you say, if I told you that Mr. Forley was only waiting for my report, to send me here next Monday, at dusk, with a bigger bit of business for us two to do together than ever you think for? What should you say to that?"

The old wretch came so near to Trottle, before she answered, and jammed him up confidentially so close into the corner of the landing, that his throat, in a manner, rose at her.

"Can you count it off, do you think, on more than that?" says she, holding up her four skinny fingers and her long crooked thumb, all of a tremble, right before his face.

"What do you say to two hands, instead of one?" says he, pushing past her, and getting down-stairs as fast as he could.

What she said Trottle thinks it best not to report, seeing that the old hypocrite, getting next door to light-headed at the golden prospect before her, took such liberties with unearthly names and persons which ought never to have approached her lips, and rained down such an awful shower of blessings on Trottle's head, that his hair almost stood on end to hear her. He went on down-stairs as fast as his feet would carry him, till he was brought up all standing, as the sailors say, on the last flight, by agravating Benjamin, lying right across the stair, and fallen off, as might have been expected, into a heavy drunken sleep.

The sight of him instantly reminded Trottle of the curious half likeness which he had already detected between the face of Benjamin and the face of another man, whom he had seen at a past time in very different circumstances. He determined, before leaving the House, to have one more look at the wretched muddled creature; and accordingly shook him up smartly, and propped him against the staircase wall, before his mother could interfere.

"Leave him to me; I'll freshen him up," says Trottle to the old woman, looking hard in Benjamin's face, while he spoke.

The fright and surprise of being suddenly woke up, seemed, for about a quarter of a minute, to sober the creature. When he first opened his eyes, there was a new look in them for a moment, which struck home to Trottle's memory as quick and as clear as a flash of light. The old maudlin sleepy expression came back again in another instant, and blurred out all further signs and tokens of the past. But Trottle had seen enough in the moment before it came; and he troubled Benjamin's face with no more inquiries.

"Next Monday, at dusk," says he, cutting short some more of the

99

old woman's palaver about Benjamin's indisgestion. "I've got no more time to spare, ma'am, to-night: please to let me out."

With a few last blessings, a few last dutiful messages to good Mr. Forley, and a few last friendly hints not to forget next Monday at dusk, Trottle contrived to struggle through the sickening business of leave-taking; to get the door opened; and to find himself, to his own indescribable relief, once more on the outer side of the House To Let.

LET AT LAST

"There, ma'am!" said Trottle, folding up the manuscript from which he had been reading, and setting it down with a smart tap of triumph on the table. "May I venture to ask what you think of that plain statement, as a guess on my part (and not on Mr. Jarber's) at the riddle of the empty House?"

For a minute or two I was unable to say a word. When I recovered a little, my first question referred to the poor forlorn little boy.

"To-day is Monday the twentieth," I said. "Surely you have not let a whole week go by without trying to find out something more?"

"Except at bed-time, and meals, ma'am," answered Trottle, "I have not let an hour go by. Please to understand that I have only come to an end of what I have written, and not to an end of what I have done. I wrote down those first particulars, ma'am, because they are of great importance, and also because I was determined to come forward with my written documents, seeing that Mr. Jarber chose to come forward, in the first instance, with his. I am now ready to go on with the second part of my story as shortly and plainly as possible, by word of mouth. The first thing I must clear up, if you please, is the matter of Mr. Forley's family affairs. I have heard you speak of them, ma'am, at various times; and I have understood that Mr. Forley had two children only by his deceased wife, both daughters. The eldest daughter married, to her father's entire satisfaction, one Mr. Bayne, a rich man, holding a high government situation in Canada. She is now living there with her husband, and her only child, a little girl of eight or nine years old. Right so far, I think, ma'am?"

"Quite right," I said.

"The second daughter," Trottle went on, "and Mr. Forley's favourite, set her father's wishes and the opinions of the world at flat defiance, by running away with a man of low origin—a mate of a merchant-vessel, named Kirkland. Mr. Forley not only never forgave that marriage, but vowed that he would visit the scandal of it heavily in the future on husband and wife. Both escaped his vengeance, whatever he meant it to be. The husband was drowned on his first voyage after his marriage, and the wife died in child-bed. Right again, I believe, ma'am?"

"Again quite right."

"Having got the family matter all right, we will now go back, ma'am, to me and my doings. Last Monday, I asked you for leave of absence for two days; I employed the time in clearing up the matter of Benjamin's face. Last Saturday I was out of the way when you wanted me. I played truant, ma'am, on that occasion, in company with a friend of mine, who is managing clerk in a lawyer's office; and we both spent the morning at Doctors' Commons, over the last will and testament of Mr. Forley's father. Leaving the will-business for a moment, please to follow me first, if you have no objection, into the ugly subject of Benjamin's face. About six or seven years ago (thanks to your kindness) I had a week's holiday with some friends of mine who live in the town of Pendlebury. One of those friends (the only one now left in the place) kept a chemist's shop, and in that shop I was made acquainted with one of the two doctors in the town, named Barsham. This Barsham was a first-rate surgeon, and might have got to the top of his profession, if he had not been a first-rate blackguard. As it was, he both drank and gambled; nobody would have anything to do with him in Pendlebury; and, at the time when I was made known to him in the chemist's shop, the other doctor, Mr. Dix, who was not to be compared with him for surgical skill, but who was a respectable man,

102

had got all the practice; and Barsham and his old mother were living together in such a condition of utter poverty, that it was a marvel to everybody how they kept out of the parish workhouse."

"Benjamin and Benjamin's mother!"

"Exactly, ma'am. Last Thursday morning (thanks to your kindness, again) I went to Pendlebury to my friend the chemist, to ask a few questions about Barsham and his mother. I was told that they had both left the town about five years since. When I inquired into the circumstances, some strange particulars came out in the course of the chemist's answer. You know I have no doubt, ma'am, that poor Mrs. Kirkland was confined while her husband was at sea, in lodgings at a village called Flatfield, and that she died and was buried there. But what you may not know is, that Flatfield is only three miles from Pendlebury; that the doctor who attended on Mrs. Kirkland was Barsham; that the nurse who took care of her was Barsham's mother; and that the person who called them both in, was Mr. Forley. Whether his daughter wrote to him, or whether he heard of it in some other way, I don't know; but he was with her (though he had sworn never to see her again when she married) a month or more before her confinement, and was backwards and forwards a good deal between Flatfield and Pendlebury. How he managed matters with the Barshams cannot at present be discovered; but it is a fact that he contrived to keep the drunken doctor sober, to everybody's amazement. It is a fact that Barsham went to the poor woman with all his wits about him. It is a fact that he and his mother came back from Flatfield after Mrs. Kirkland's death, packed up what few things they had, and left the town mysteriously by night. And, lastly, it is also a fact that the other doctor, Mr. Dix, was not called in to help, till a week after the birth *and burial* of the child, when the mother was sinking from exhaustion—exhaustion (to give the vagabond, Barsham, his due) not produced, in Mr. Dix's opinion, by improper medical treatment, but by the bodily weakness of the poor woman herself—"

"Burial of the child?" I interrupted, trembling all over. "Trottle! you spoke that word 'burial' in a very strange way—you are fixing your eyes on me now with a very strange look—"

Trottle leaned over close to me, and pointed through the window to the empty house.

"The child's death is registered, at Pendlebury," he said, "on Barsham's certificate, under the head of Male Infant, Still-Born. The child's coffin lies in the mother's grave, in Flatfield churchyard. The child himself—as surely as I live and breathe, is living and breathing now—a castaway and a prisoner in that villainous house!"

I sank back in my chair.

"It's guess-work, so far, but it is borne in on my mind, for all that, as truth. Rouse yourself, ma'am, and think a little. The last I hear of Barsham, he is attending Mr. Forley's disobedient daughter. The next I see of Barsham, he is in Mr. Forley's house, trusted with a secret. He and his mother leave Pendlebury suddenly and suspiciously five years back; and he and his mother have got a child of five years old, hidden away in the house. Wait! please to wait—I have not done yet. The will left by Mr. Forley's father, strengthens the suspicion. The friend I took with me to Doctors' Commons, made himself master of the contents of that will; and when he had done so, I put these two questions to him. 'Can Mr. Forley leave his money at his own discretion to anybody he pleases?' 'No,' my friend says, 'his father has left him with only a life interest in it.' 'Suppose one of Mr. Forley's married daughters has a girl, and the other a boy, how would the money go?' 'It would all go,' my friend says, 'to the boy, and it would be charged with the payment of a certain annual income to his female cousin. After her death, it would go

104

back to the male descendant, and to his heirs.' Consider that, ma'am! The child of the daughter whom Mr. Forley hates, whose husband has been snatched away from his vengeance by death, takes his whole property in defiance of him; and the child of the daughter whom he loves, is left a pensioner on her low-born boy-cousin for life! There was good—too good reason—why that child of Mrs. Kirkland's should be registered stillborn. And if, as I believe, the register is founded on a false certificate, there is better, still better reason, why the existence of the child should be hidden, and all trace of his parentage blotted out, in the garret of that empty house."

He stopped, and pointed for the second time to the dim, dust-covered garret-windows opposite. As he did so, I was startled—a very slight matter sufficed to frighten me now—by a knock at the door of the room in which we were sitting.

My maid came in, with a letter in her hand. I took it from her. The mourning card, which was all the envelope enclosed, dropped from my hands.

George Forley was no more. He had departed this life three days since, on the evening of Friday.

"Did our last chance of discovering the truth," I asked, "rest with *him*? Has it died with *his* death?"

"Courage, ma'am! I think not. Our chance rests on our power to make Barsham and his mother confess; and Mr. Forley's death, by leaving them helpless, seems to put that power into our hands. With your permission, I will not wait till dusk to-day, as I at first intended, but will make sure of those two people at once. With a policeman in plain clothes to watch the house, in case they try to leave it; with this card to vouch for the fact of Mr. Forley's death; and with a bold acknowledgment on my part of having got possession of their secret, and of being ready to use it against them in case of need, I think there is little doubt of

105

bringing Barsham and his mother to terms. In case I find it impossible to get back here before dusk, please to sit near the window, ma'am, and watch the house, a little before they light the street-lamps. If you see the front-door open and close again, will you be good enough to put on your bonnet, and come across to me immediately? Mr. Forley's death may, or may not, prevent his messenger from coming as arranged. But, if the person does come, it is of importance that you, as a relative of Mr. Forley's should be present to see him, and to have that proper influence over him which I cannot pretend to exercise."

The only words I could say to Trottle as he opened the door and left me, were words charging him to take care that no harm happened to the poor forlorn little boy.

Left alone, I drew my chair to the window; and looked out with a beating heart at the guilty house. I waited and waited through what appeared to me to be an endless time, until I heard the wheels of a cab stop at the end of the street. I looked in that direction, and saw Trottle get out of the cab alone, walk up to the house, and knock at the door. He was let in by Barsham's mother. A minute or two later, a decently-dressed man sauntered past the house, looked up at it for a moment, and sauntered on to the corner of the street close by. Here he leant against the post, and lighted a cigar, and stopped there smoking in an idle way, but keeping his face always turned in the direction of the house-door.

I waited and waited still. I waited and waited, with my eyes riveted to the door of the house. At last I thought I saw it open in the dusk, and then felt sure I heard it shut again softly. Though I tried hard to compose myself, I trembled so that I was obliged to call for Peggy to help me on with my bonnet and cloak, and was forced to take her arm to lean on, in crossing the street.

Trottle opened the door to us, before we could knock. Peggy

went back, and I went in. He had a lighted candle in his hand.

"It has happened, ma'am, as I thought it would," he whispered, leading me into the bare, comfortless, empty parlour. "Barsham and his mother have consulted their own interests, and have come to terms. My guess-work is guess-work no longer. It is now what I felt it was—Truth!"

Something strange to me—something which women who are mothers must often know—trembled suddenly in my heart, and brought the warm tears of my youthful days thronging back into my eyes. I took my faithful old servant by the hand, and asked him to let me see Mrs. Kirkland's child, for his mother's sake.

"If you desire it, ma'am," said Trottle, with a gentleness of manner that I had never noticed in him before. "But pray don't think me wanting in duty and right feeling, if I beg you to try and wait a little. You are agitated already, and a first meeting with the child will not help to make you so calm, as you would wish to be, if Mr. Forley's messenger comes. The little boy is safe up-stairs. Pray think first of trying to compose yourself for a meeting with a stranger; and believe me you shall not leave the house afterwards without the child."

I felt that Trottle was right, and sat down as patiently as I could in a chair he had thoughtfully placed ready for me. I was so horrified at the discovery of my own relation's wickedness that when Trottle proposed to make me acquainted with the confession wrung from Barsham and his mother, I begged him to spare me all details, and only to tell me what was necessary about George Forley.

"All that can be said for Mr. Forley, ma'am, is, that he was just scrupulous enough to hide the child's existence and blot out its parentage here, instead of consenting, at the first, to its death, or afterwards, when the boy grew up, to turning him adrift, absolutely helpless in the world. The fraud has been managed, ma'am, with the cunning of Satan himself. Mr. Forley had the hold over the Barshams, that they had helped him in his villany, and that they were dependent on him for the bread they eat. He brought them up to London to keep them securely under his own eye. He put them into this empty house (taking it out of the agent's hands previously, on pretence that he meant to manage the letting of it himself); and by keeping the house empty, made it the surest of all hiding places for the child. Here, Mr. Forley could come, whenever he pleased, to see that the poor lonely child was not absolutely starved; sure that his visits would only appear like looking after his own property. Here the child was to have been trained to believe himself Barsham's child, till he should be old enough to be provided for in some situation, as low and as poor as Mr. Forley's uneasy conscience would let him pick out. He may have thought of atonement on his death-bed; but not before—I am only too certain of it—not before!"

A low, double knock startled us.

"The messenger!" said Trottle, under his breath. He went out instantly to answer the knock; and returned, leading in a respectable-looking elderly man, dressed like Trottle, all in black, with a white cravat, but otherwise not at all resembling him.

"I am afraid I have made some mistake," said the stranger.

Trottle, considerately taking the office of explanation into his own hands, assured the gentleman that there was no mistake; mentioned to him who I was; and asked him if he had not come on business connected with the late Mr. Forley. Looking greatly astonished, the gentleman answered, "Yes." There was an awkward moment of silence, after that. The stranger seemed to be not only startled and amazed, but rather distrustful and fearful of committing himself as well. Noticing this, I thought it best to request Trottle to put an end to further embarrassment, by stating all particulars truthfully, as he had stated them to me;

and I begged the gentleman to listen patiently for the late Mr. Forley's sake. He bowed to me very respectfully, and said he was prepared to listen with the greatest interest.

It was evident to me—and, I could see, to Trottle also—that we were not dealing, to say the least, with a dishonest man.

"Before I offer any opinion on what I have heard," he said, earnestly and anxiously, after Trottle had done, "I must be allowed, in justice to myself, to explain my own apparent connection with this very strange and very shocking business. I was the confidential legal adviser of the late Mr. Forley, and I am left his executor. Rather more than a fortnight back, when Mr. Forley was confined to his room by illness, he sent for me, and charged me to call and pay a certain sum of money here, to a man and woman whom I should find taking charge of the house. He said he had reasons for wishing the affair to be kept a secret. He begged me so to arrange my engagements that I could call at this place either on Monday last, or to-day, at dusk; and he mentioned that he would write to warn the people of my coming, without mentioning my name (Dalcott is my name), as he did not wish to expose me to any future importunities on the part of the man and woman. I need hardly tell you that this commission struck me as being a strange one; but, in my position with Mr. Forley, I had no resource but to accept it without asking questions, or to break off my long and friendly connection with my client. I chose the first alternative. Business prevented me from doing my errand on Monday last—and if I am here to-day, notwithstanding Mr. Forley's unexpected death, it is emphatically because I understood nothing of the matter, on knocking at this door; and therefore felt myself bound, as executor, to clear it up. That, on my word of honour, is the whole truth, so far as I am personally concerned."

"I feel quite sure of it, sir," I answered.

"You mentioned Mr. Forley's death, just now, as

unexpected. May I inquire if you were present, and if he has left any last instructions?"

"Three hours before Mr. Forley's death," said Mr. Dalcott, "his medical attendant left him apparently in a fair way of recovery. The change for the worse took place so suddenly, and was accompanied by such severe suffering, to prevent him from communicating his last wishes to any one. When I reached his house, he was insensible. I have since examined his papers. Not one of them refers to the present time or to the serious matter which now occupies us. In the absence of instructions I must act cautiously on what you have told me; but I will be rigidly fair and just at the same time. The first thing to be done," he continued, addressing himself to Trottle, "is to hear what the man and woman, down-stairs, have to say. If you can supply me with writing-materials, I will take their declarations separately on the spot, in your presence, and in the presence of the policeman who is watching the house. To-morrow I will send copies of those declarations, accompanied by a full statement of the case, to Mr. and Mrs. Bayne in Canada (both of whom know me well as the late Mr. Forley's legal adviser); and I will suspend all proceedings, on my part, until I hear from them, or from their solicitor in London. In the present posture of affairs this is all I can safely do."

We could do no less than agree with him, and thank him for his frank and honest manner of meeting us. It was arranged that I should send over the writing-materials from my lodgings; and, to my unutterable joy and relief, it was also readily acknowledged that the poor little orphan boy could find no fitter refuge than my old arms were longing to offer him, and no safer protection for the night than my roof could give. Trottle hastened away up-stairs, as actively as if he had been a young man, to fetch the child down.

And he brought him down to me without another moment of

110

delay, and I went on my knees before the poor little Mite, and embraced him, and asked him if he would go with me to where I lived? He held me away for a moment, and his wan, shrewd little eyes looked sharp at me. Then he clung close to me all at once, and said:

"I'm a-going along with you, I am—and so I tell you!"

For inspiring the poor neglected child with this trust in my old self, I thanked Heaven, then, with all my heart and soul, and I thank it now!

I bundled the poor darling up in my own cloak, and I carried him in my own arms across the road. Peggy was lost in speechless amazement to behold me trudging out of breath upstairs, with a strange pair of poor little legs under my arm; but, she began to cry over the child the moment she saw him, like a sensible woman as she always was, and she still cried her eyes out over him in a comfortable manner, when he at last lay fast asleep, tucked up by my hands in Trottle's bed.

"And Trottle, bless you, my dear man," said I, kissing his hand, as he looked on: "the forlorn baby came to this refuge through you, and he will help you on your way to Heaven."

Trottle answered that I was his dear mistress, and immediately went and put his head out at an open window on the landing, and looked into the back street for a quarter of an hour.

That very night, as I sat thinking of the poor child, and of another poor child who is never to be thought about enough at Christmas-time, the idea came into my mind which I have lived to execute, and in the realisation of which I am the happiest of women this day.

"The executor will sell that House, Trottle?" said I.

"Not a doubt of it, ma'am, if he can find a purchaser."

111

"I'll buy it."

I have often seen Trottle pleased; but, I never saw him so perfectly enchanted as he was when I confided to him, which I did, then and there, the purpose that I had in view.

To make short of a long story—and what story would not be long, coming from the lips of an old woman like me, unless it was made short by main force!—I bought the House. Mrs. Bayne had her father's blood in her; she evaded the opportunity of forgiving and generous reparation that was offered her, and disowned the child; but, I was prepared for that, and loved him all the more for having no one in the world to look to, but me.

I am getting into a flurry by being over-pleased, and I dare say I am as incoherent as need be. I bought the House, and I altered it from the basement to the roof, and I turned it into a Hospital for Sick Children.

Never mind by what degrees my little adopted boy came to the knowledge of all the sights and sounds in the streets, so familiar to other children and so strange to him; never mind by what degrees he came to be pretty, and childish, and winning, and companionable, and to have pictures and toys about him, and suitable playmates. As I write, I look across the road to my Hospital, and there is the darling (who has gone over to play) nodding at me out of one of the once lonely windows, with his dear chubby face backed up by Trottle's waistcoat as he lifts my pet for "Grandma" to see.

Many an Eye I see in that House now, but it is never in solitude, never in neglect. Many an Eye I see in that House now, that is more and more radiant every day with the light of returning health. As my precious darling has changed beyond description for the brighter and the better, so do the not less precious darlings of poor women change in that House every day in the year. For which I humbly thank that Gracious Being whom the restorer of the Widow's son and of the Ruler's daughter, instructed all mankind to call their Father.

www.ingramcontent.com/pod-product-compliance
Lightning Source LLC
Chambersburg PA
CBHW011440170626
46807CB00008B/3249